DEFYING CONVENTION
WOMEN WHO CHANGED THE RULES

WOMEN ATHLETES

SHERRI MABRY GORDON

Enslow Publishing
101 W. 23rd Street
Suite 240
New York, NY 10011
USA

enslow.com

Published in 2017 by Enslow Publishing, LLC.
101 W. 23rd Street, Suite 240, New York, NY 10011

Library of Congress Cataloging-in-Publication Data

Names: Gordon, Sherri Mabry, author.
Title: Women athletes / Sherri Mabry Gordon.
Description: New York, NY : Enslow Publishing, 2017. | Series: Defying convention : women who changed the rules | Includes bibliographical references and index.
Identifiers: LCCN 2016026261 | ISBN 9780766081475 (library bound)
Subjects: LCSH: Women athletes—History—Juvenile literature. | Sports for women—History—Juvenile literature.
Classification: LCC GV709 .G59 2017 | DDC 796.082—dc23
LC record available at https://lccn.loc.gov/2016026261

Printed in Malaysia

To Our Readers: We have done our best to make sure all websites in this book were active and appropriate when we went to press. However, the author and the publisher have no control over and assume no liability for the material available on those websites or on any websites they may link to. Any comments or suggestions can be sent by e-mail to customerservice@enslow.com.

CONTENTS

Kacy Stuart never knew being a girl could keep her from playing the sport she loved. Before her family moved and she joined the football team at a private school, Kacy was a kicker for another school in Georgia. It was there that she was welcomed by the team and played the sport she loved.

She recounts memories of feeling the ground beneath her shaking, the crowd stomping and shouting as she took the field to kick another game-winner. It was there that she experienced the bench clearing at the end of a game and the rest of the football players gathering around her in celebration, never bothered by the fact that she was a girl. She was simply part of the team.[1]

It never occurred to Kacy that her experience at a new school would be different. But it was vastly different. Not long after the season started at her new school, the Georgia Football League informed Kacy that she could not play football in the league. Their explanation was simple: "You are a girl." No other reason was given, just that. You are a girl and you cannot play football.[2]

Fortunately, in Kacy's situation, this ban from the sport she loved was short-lived. It was not long before she was reinstated and allowed to play football again. But not all girls have the same experience. Some are told they

Even though girls and women have proven they can be talented athletes and fierce competitors, stereotypes persist that being physical is not feminine.

cannot play, and they never push back. They simply walk away, leaving their dreams of competing to die in the dust.

Girls are bombarded by gender stereotypes from birth. Aside from being dressed in pink as babies, young girls are often instructed to be lady-like and not to demonstrate any characteristics that might be considered masculine. These gender stereotypes are especially evident when it comes to

Historically, girls and women have been deemed the weaker sex physically, mentally, and emotionally. As a result, girls were often discouraged from participating in sports because sweating, grunting, and being aggressive were not considered attractive or feminine. What's more, many people felt the female body simply could not handle physical exertion.

For instance, in 1896 Baron Pierre de Coubertin, founder of the modern Olympics stated: "No matter how toughened a sportswoman may be her organism is not cut out to sustain certain shocks."[3]

And although there has been a lot of progress in knocking down these barriers, women today still face challenges when it comes to participating in sports. For instance, they do not always have the same opportunities and incentives.

What's more, girls are still ridiculed or called names if they are athletic and are often accused of being a lesbian or appearing manly. Consequently, it should come as no surprise that even today, girls are six times more likely than their male counterparts to stop participating in sports by the time they turn fourteen.[4]

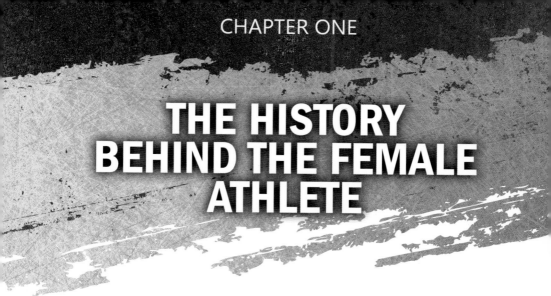

CHAPTER ONE

THE HISTORY BEHIND THE FEMALE ATHLETE

For centuries, athletics, team competitions, and sporting events were considered part of a man's world and not open to women. As a result, many girls and women not only avoided taking part in sports, but also refrained from attending sporting events. If they did participate in any type of physical activity, it was often limited to culturally "accept-able" activities, such as dancing and ice-skating.

By the mid-1800s women started attending sport-ing events, such as horse races and baseball games. And by the late 1800s, women began to participate in some organized sports, such as golf, archery, and croquet. These activities were accepted by society at the time because they were not too physical and did not require a woman to exert herself too much.[1]

But a female's ability to participate in sports was still very limited. Sweating and physical activity was still frowned upon. What's more, women were required to "protect their reproductive systems."[2]

Before the nineteenth century came to a close, women began to ride bikes more and more frequently. This fact led to many changes for women. They began to participate in more physical activities and started dressing differently. Their new clothing allowed easier movement so that they could enjoy riding both bicycles and horses. This cultural shift also allowed women to participate in sports. It liberated them in attire, roles, and professions.[3]

In fact, Susan B. Anthony, the leader of the women's suffrage movement, said: "Let me tell you what I think of bicycling. I think it has done more to emancipate women than anything else in the world. I stand and rejoice every time I see a woman ride by on a wheel."[4]

BREAKING DOWN BARRIERS

With these revolutionary changes, the barriers keeping women from participating in sports began to crumble. Although discrimination was still evident, women continued to push forward. As a result, this time period still featured many accomplishments by female athletes.[5] Among the many remarkable achievements are those of Babe Didrikson Zaharias and Jackie Mitchell.

After World War II, female participation in competitive sports continued to grow. By the 1960s and 1970s, the women's movement was

Women's tennis champion Billie Jean King accepted a challenge from retired pro player Bobby Riggs in 1973. King proved that women athletes were not inferior to males, defeating Riggs handily.

gaining momentum. People were developing new attitudes about women. In addition to equal rights, they also wanted equal funding and equal facilities for women who participated in sports.[6]

During this time, one of the most famous tennis matches ever took place. Often referred to as the "Battle of the Sexes," Billie Jean King took on Bobby Riggs, a former men's champion. When King won, this victory was also a victory for women's sports. Despite the discrimination that women faced and the unfounded perceptions about a woman's ability to excel in sports, women continued to push forward and prove the world wrong.

SAVING LIVES

During the 2004 tsunami in Indonesia, many women and girls were injured or drowned because they did not know how to swim. They also had no idea how to climb onto roofs, climb trees, or find other safe areas like the men and boys in their community. Consequently, countless female lives were lost because they did not know how to save themselves.

As a result, Women Without Borders, together with the Austrian Swimming Association and the Austrian Life-Saving Federation, began offering swimming lessons to girls and women in the areas along the coast. This program prepares them for survival, especially if another tsunami hits. What's more, it builds self-confidence and develops a sense of community and belonging among the women. Additionally, it will help build respect for women within their communities.[7]

SPORTS AND EMPOWERMENT

The relationship between equal rights and athletics is not just about giving girls and women the same opportunities as boys and men. It also is not about being treated fairly. It is about using sports to empower girls. As Myriam Lamare, a World Boxing Association champion from France, has pointed out, "the punches [a girl] lands shake the foundations of society."[8]

Sports also provide a way to challenge stereotypes and put an end to discrimination. When women participate in sports and are successful,

For much of history, the only acceptable physical activities for women were those considered feminine, such as figure skating and dance. Today, women participate in sports of all kinds, including boxing.

this destroys myths about what women are capable of. It also influences their roles in their community. Likewise, when women have more leadership roles in the athletic community, this can change attitudes about their abilities to be athletes, leaders, and decision makers.

One example is Nawal El Moutawakel, who runs hurdles in Morocco. Moutawakel knows that she is a role model for women, especially Muslim women, and says that her main function as a member of the IOC is "to encourage more women to participate in sport worldwide."[9]

Sports teach girls and women important skills, including teamwork, negotiation, communication, and respect for others. They also serve to build self-esteem and self-confidence. What's more, women and girls who play sports have lower levels of depression and often go on to have successful careers. For instance, in a recent study of female executives at Fortune 500 companies, 80 percent described themselves as "tomboys."[10]

Finally, participating in sports allows women and girls to express themselves through movement. This increases self-esteem and builds self-confidence. Girls develop an awareness and an understanding of their bodies. They also feel more ownership over their bodies and have more self-respect.

In fact, the Women's Sports Foundation recently studied the connection between sports and teen pregnancy in the United States. They found that girls who play sports have more ownership of and respect for their bodies. In turn, this leads to delayed sexual activity.

Research by the Wellesley Centers for Women also found links between sports and girls' sexual behavior. The study showed a decrease in risky sexual behavior among girls who participate in sports. What it discovered was that the delay in sexual initiation was partly due to a healthy self-esteem. Other contributing factors were a less stereotypical gender identity and a stronger desire to avoid teenage pregnancy.[11]

Overall, the potential for sports participation to impact the social, economic, and political empowerment of women and girls is clear. Many governments around the world, as well as the United Nations, recognize this fact. The next step is to bring the benefits of sports and physical education to every woman and girl in the world.[12]

ADDITIONAL FACTS ABOUT GIRLS AND SPORTS

- By the age of fourteen, girls drop out of sports six times more often than boys.
- Boys have twice the number of sports participation opportunities in high school and college.

- Girls often start participating in sports two years later than boys.
- If a girl is not playing sports by the time she is ten years old, there is less than a 10 percent chance she will be playing when she is twenty-five.
- High school girls who play sports are less likely to have an unwanted pregnancy. They are also less likely to be involved with drugs and more likely to graduate from high school.
- One to three hours of exercise a week can bring a 20 to 30 percent reduction in the risk of breast cancer. Meanwhile, four or more hours of exercise a week can reduce the risk by almost 60 percent.
- Generations of women that were not permitted to play sports or participate in weight-bearing exercises are now dealing with bone mass issues. Half of women over the age of sixty suffers from osteoporosis.
- Girls and women who play sports have higher levels of self-esteem and self-confidence, stronger self-images, and lower levels of depression.
- In a recent study of female executives at Fortune 500 companies, 80 percent self-identified as having been "tomboys."[13]

CHAPTER TWO

HISTORY OF THE OLYMPICS AND WOMEN

The road to equality for women at the Olympic Games has been a long one. Still, women push against the barriers and each time pave the way for the female athletes who will follow them.

The Olympic Games, in particular, have a long history of excluding women from the games. When the first Olympics were held in Greece in 776 BCE, men were so bent on keeping women from having anything to do with the games that they even prohibited them from watching the games.

The law said that if a woman attended the games, she would be thrown from the cliffs of Mount Typaion. Although this law was harsh, there is no record that it was ever enforced. But one woman broke the law.

Her name was Kallipateira. She dressed like a trainer to watch her son in the boxing competition. During the awards, Kallipateira ran out to congratulate her son. When she greeted him, the crowd saw her identity. But because she was from a noble family, she went unpunished. After that, though, trainers were nude so that women could not sneak in undetected. What's more, to ensure that males were the ones competing, athletes also were nude.[1]

In response to the ban on women in the ancient Olympics, the Games of Hera were organized for female athletes. These games were dedicated to the wife of Zeus. They began as foot races among girls of different ages. The games took place in the same stadium as the men's Olympics.

However, the foot races were shortened by one-sixth of what the men were running. Winners received a crown made of olive branches and a share of the cow or ox sacrificed to Hera. Statues containing their names were also distributed.[2]

THE FIRST WOMAN OLYMPIAN

Kyniska was from Sparta and bred horses on a regular basis. At one point, historians note that she entered them in the tethrippon, which was a prestigious horse race. The rules stated that, "the owner and master of the horses who won the tethrippon was the winner of that event." But it did not specifically exclude women. Because horse racing was costly, the issue of gender was never considered. When Kyniska entered her horses in the race, no one expected her to win. But she did.

This fact made Kyniska the first women to compete in and win an Olympic sport. She tried again at the next Olympics and won again. But she was not allowed to enter the stadium for the awards. However, she is still listed as an Olympic winner.

Later, she was permitted to place her statute in Zeus's sanctuary. The statue's inscription said: "I declare myself the only woman in all Hellas [Greece] to have won this crown." Kyniska's win at the "all male" Olympics set a model for women in the future to enter the Olympics under the same types of loopholes.[3]

WOMEN AT THE OLYMPIC GAMES

In 1896, a Greek woman named Stamata Revithi wanted to run the Olympic marathon. When the local priest refused to bless her before the race, the organizing committee said she could not compete. Still, Revithi ran the race, completing it in five and a half hours. But she was turned away at the stadium entrance and not allowed to enter.

Other historians mention a woman known as Melpomene, who completed the marathon in four and a half hours. Some believe that

Revithi and Melpomene were the same person. Regardless, Pierre de Coubertin, the father of the modern Olympics, said he did not like the idea of women running in the games: "It is indecent that the spectators should be exposed to the risk of seeing the body of a woman being smashed before their very eyes," he said.[4] "Her organism is not cut out to sustain certain shocks." He also said that women's "primary role should be to crown the victors."[5]

As a result, women continued to face significant barriers to participating in Olympic competition. To combat this issue, Frenchwoman Alice Milliat organized a separate Women's Olympic Games in 1922. However, the IOC did not want a separate Olympics so it started to offer greater opportunities for women.[6]

Once women were permitted to participate in the modern Olympics, they were not well represented. In the 1900 Olympics, the first nineteen women competed in just three sports. These included tennis, golf, and croquet. By the 2004 Olympic Games, women competed in twenty-six out of twenty-eight sports. This figure represented 40.7 percent of the total number of athletes in the Olympics. It also set a record for women's participation in the Olympic Games.[7]

Prior to the 2012 Olympics, Qatar, Brunei, and Saudi Arabia had never before sent a female

Women ran the 800-meter sprint in Monte Carlo in preparation for the 1922 Women's World Games. These tournaments were organized to compensate for the lack of Olympic events for women.

athlete. But in 2012, this changed. This was the first Olympics in which all of the participating countries sent female athletes. What's more, Qatar's air-rifle shooter, Bahiya al Hamad, carried her country's flag at the opening ceremonies. And in 2016 the US team sent 294 female athletes compared to 264 men.[8]

The International Olympic Committee allowed a limited number of women's events in the 1928 games in Amsterdam, including the 100-meter sprint.

ONE STEP FORWARD AND A FEW STEPS BACK

In the 1928 Olympics, women were allowed to participate in five track and field events for the first time. This was done on a trial basis. The events included the 100-meter and 800-meter races, the 4 x 100-meter relay race, the running high jump, and the discus.

Nine female runners took to the track to compete in the 800-meter finals. It was the longest race at the time, and many people thought it was too difficult for women. When the race was over, some of the runners dropped to their knees on the infield. This scared the officials, and they rushed out in a panic to administer first aid.

Collapsing at the end of a big race is not uncommon. But the male officials and reporters felt this proved that 800 meters was too much for women to handle.

As a result, the all-male International Amateur Athletic Federation (IAAF) banned all women's races longer than 200 meters. This ban lasted thirty-two years. In 1960, the 800-meter was finally reinstated. Although the IAAF argued that its decision was a humanitarian one, many felt that the federation was trying to exert power over women, making their choices for them.

It wasn't until 1981 that the IOC voted to allow women to compete in marathons. This was in large part due to Kathrine Switzer, who ran the Boston Marathon amid protest from the race's director.

It has not been an easy path for women when it comes to competing in the Olympics and athletics in general. So if you are a female and enjoy running, by all means run. Today, it is unlikely you will be told that it is not ladylike or too strenuous. Instead, you just might be encouraged to run. Most would agree that exercise is best for you and your body.[9]

IMPORTANT FEMALE OLYMPIC ACHIEVEMENTS

- In 1948, Dutch athlete Fanny Blankers-Koen won four gold medals. This is equivalent to the medals Jesse Owens had won twelve years earlier. She also held the world record in the high and long jumps. But she did not compete in those events. The rules prohibited women from competing in more than three individual events.
- British equestrian Lorna Johnstone was seventy years old when she rode at the 1972 games. As a result, she was the oldest woman ever to compete at an Olympic Games.
- American Joan Benoit won the very first women's Olympic marathon in 1984.
- Soviet Maria Gorokhovskaya set a record in 1952 for the most medals won by a woman in one Olympics. She won two gold medals and five silvers.
- In 1976, US shooter Margaret Murdock won a silver medal in rifle competition (which at that time included both men and women). This made her the first woman to win a medal in shooting at the Olympic Games.[10]
- Swimmer Katie Ledecky became the most decorated female athlete of the 2016 games in Rio, winning four gold medals, one silver, and two world records.

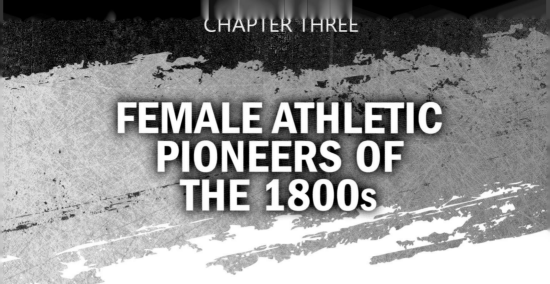

CHAPTER THREE

FEMALE ATHLETIC PIONEERS OF THE 1800s

I f you love playing sports and being active, you have something in common with a lot of the women profiled in this book. But although it's considered normal for women to be athletic today, there was a time when physical activity was considered a masculine activity and immoral for girls.

Sweating, in particular, was considered unladylike and offensive. According to society's rules, female exercise was an assault to a woman's role as a mother. As a result, female participation in sports was prohibited.

Conventional wisdom said that physical activity would damage reproduction. However, this assumption was never based on scientific evidence. Other commonly held views included that female participation in sports was unnatural, damaging, and just plain gross.

Yet, despite being prohibited from participating in athletics, the invention of the bicycle in the late 1800s helped advance women's rights, specifically in sports.

Changes in women's fashion had an impact on athletics, as well. Many women of the time enjoyed wearing bloomers, a daring-for-the-time garment inspired by Turkish pants. Bloomers were named after Amelia Bloomer. They were quickly adopted by suffragists, such as Susan B. Anthony, and became common attire for women who rode bicycles. Bloomers were less restricting and provided more physical freedom.

These changes in societal attitudes, combined with the efforts of many courageous women who fought against the conviction that sports should be limited to boys and men, helped open doors for women in sports today. Several of the more notable early pioneers for female sports participation include Alicia Meynell, Ellen Hansell and Charlotte "Lottie" Dod.

ALICIA MEYNELL (1782–?)

Alicia Meynell, born in 1782, became the first female jockey. She competed in a 4-mile (6.4-km) horse race in York, England, in 1804. The race was the result of an argument between Meynell and her brother-in-law, Captain William Flint. After riding one day, the two began to argue over who had the better horse. They raced on the spot that day, and Meynell won, but Flint challenged her to a proper race on a real track.

The day of the race brought many spectators to see a woman race a horse. And Meynell did not disappoint them. She showed up to the race in a dress designed to look like leopard skin, with blue sleeves, a buff-colored vest, and a blue cap. The crowd had to be restrained by the 6th Light Dragoons. More than 200,000 pounds (more than $6 million today) was bet that day.[1]

Flint ordered Meynell to ride on the side of the track where she would not be able to use her whip hand. He also did not allow anyone to ride alongside her should her sidesaddle slip.[2] When the race finally started, Meynell quickly took the lead and held it for the first three miles.[3] But her horse, Vingarillo, hesitated all of a sudden. This allowed Flint's horse, Thornville, to race past him. Flint won the race. The race had lasted nine minutes and fifty-nine seconds.[4]

Most felt Meynell accepted defeat with grace and dignity, but it wasn't long before she called for a rematch. In September 1804, a letter from Meynell appeared in the *York Herald* challenging Flint to another race when she could be mounted on a better horse. She also pointed out that he did not treat her with proper courtesy because he did not allow her to have an escort should her saddle slip. Flint accepted the rematch, but the race never took place.

However, Meynell did race Buckle, the leading jockey of the day. Meynell won that race but many argued that Buckle had thrown the race in order to appear gentlemanly. Others countered that he was so honest that he would never throw a race, not even to a lady. In England's Jockey Club's records, Meynell was listed as the only woman to have raced and won against a man until 1943.[5]

ELLEN HANSELL (1869–1937)

In the summer of 1887, Philadelphia native Ellen Hansell became the first US National Women's Singles champion at the Philadelphia Cricket Club. At just seventeen years old, Hansell defeated Laura Knight in the championship match, 6–1 and 6–0. However, the following year, she was unsuccessful in defending her title and lost to Bertha Townsend, 6–3 and 6–5 in the championship match. After her loss to Townsend, Hansell was not able to win another match.[6]

US National Women's Singles champion Ellen Hansell (far right) posed with three fellow American women tennis players. From left: Bertha Townsend, Bargie Ballard, and Louise Allerdice.

Historians report that Hansell, who was born September 18, 1869, was anemic as a child but showed promising ability in tennis. Consequently, her family doctor had advised her mother to remove Ellen from school and have her play tennis all day. The goal was to help her develop a more solid build and address her anemia.

Hansell was also known for her statement-making outfits, which consisted of red plaid gingham. Basically, she wore a red felt hat on a tight-collared and corseted body, plus a blazer of blue and red stripes.[7]

Hansell retired from tennis in 1890 and dedicated herself to being a wife and a mother of six children. Her achievement as the premier ladies champion was duly recognized at the 1931 Golden Jubilee celebration of the United States Lawn Tennis Association, where she was honored alongside the first men's champion, Richard Sears.[8]

Ellen Hansell died in May of 1937 in Pittsburgh. She was inducted into the International Tennis Hall of Fame in 1965.[9]

LOTTIE DOD (1871–1960)

Charlotte "Lottie" Dod was an English tennis prodigy. At only fifteen years old, she became the

Lottie Dod was a versatile and talented athlete, excelling in such sports as golf, hockey, croquet, and archery. Dodd was introduced to tennis early and became Wimbledon champion when she was only fifteen years old.

youngest woman to win Wimbledon. She won the 1887 Wimbledon Ladies Singles Championship defeating Blanche Hillyard. Twenty-three-year-old Hillyard was the reigning champion, and Dod defeated her 6–2, 6–0. In fact, Dod was so overpowering that the second set lasted only ten minutes.[10] Dod remained the youngest women's Wimbledon champion for more than one hundred years. In 1996, Martina Hingis, who was three days younger than Dod had been at her victory, won the ladies' doubles title.[11]

Lottie Dod was born on September 24, 1871, in Cheshire, England. She was the youngest child of a wealthy cotton broker and was introduced to tennis when she was just nine years old. By 1883, she had won a consolation doubles competition with her sister, Ann, at the Northern Championships held at Manchester Lawn Tennis Club. Then in 1885, when she was thirteen, she won all three open events at the Waterloo tournament and gave the current Wimbledon champion, Maud Watson, a close contest in the All-Comers' Final of the Northern Championships before losing 8–6, 7–5.[12]

In 1887, Dod also won the Irish Nationals Singles Championship, defeating Watson 6–4, 6–3.[13] Nicknamed "the Little Wonder," Dod won four more championships in 1888, 1891, 1892, and

1893, all of which were against Blanche Hillyard. In the 1893 match, twenty-one-year-old Dod lost the first set 8–6 but then won the next two 6–1 and 6–4. In her previous four victories, Dod lost only thirteen games in all.[14]

In 1888, Dod was less dominant but even so she again defeated Hillyard at Wimbledon, in the Challenge Round, 6–3, 6–3. The match lasted under half an hour. In 1899, she was unwilling to disrupt a yachting holiday and declined to defend her title. Then in 1890, she played no championship tennis but returned to Wimbledon in 1891 and 1892. By then, her powerful volleying and overheads were untouchable. Dod retired from tennis competition in 1893 partly because of boredom and partly because of a desire to try her hand at other sports.[15]

Dod's family was wealthy and filled with athletes. Like her brothers and sisters, Dod enjoyed an independent income left to her by her father. She was educated by governesses and private tutors and enjoyed playing sports. She and her family enjoyed croquet, archery, golf, billiards, and skating.

Dod's older sister, Ann, was an accomplished skater and was considered one of the best billiards players in England. Her brother William won a gold medal for archery at the 1908 Olympic Games in London. Meanwhile, her brother Anthony was chess champion of Cheshire and Lancashire.

In addition to tennis, Dod was also accomplished in skiing, archery, field hockey, and golf. At the turn of the century, Dod made two appearances for England's hockey team. In a March 1900 match, she scored twice and impressed many with her stick work. In 1904, she became the British national golf champion. She also earned a spot on the 1908 Olympic archery team and won the silver medal.[16]

Because of her young age at the time she competed in tennis, she was allowed to wear clothing that looked like her school uniform. As a result, she wore a calf-length dress, black stockings and shoes, and a white flannel cricket cap atop her black hair. Consequently, she was able to move more freely than women wearing full-length dresses, giving her an advantage. Yet, despite the small advantage her outfit gave her, it was her skill that took her all the way. She frequently went running across court, smashed the ball, and served in a way her competitors did not.

It was certainly not a ladylike game according to the time period, but Dod made no excuses. "As a rule, ladies are too lazy at tennis," she once said. "They should learn to run and run their hardest, too, not merely stride. They would find, if they tried, that many a ball, seemingly out of reach, could be returned with ease; but instead of running hard they go a few steps and exclaim, 'Oh, I can't' and stop."[17]

Dod, who never married, passed away at the age of eighty-eight in a nursing home in June 1960. Rumor has it she was listening to the 83rd Wimbledon Championships on the radio at the time.

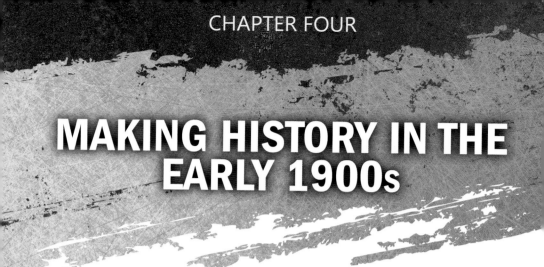

CHAPTER FOUR

MAKING HISTORY IN THE EARLY 1900s

I n the early 1900s, people still believed that physical activity would endanger a woman's reproductive capabilities as well as produce unsightly muscle. The fear was that women would no longer appear feminine and ladylike, nor would they be able to bear children. As a result, early sports for women and girls were often limited to archery, dancing, croquet, golf, swimming, and tennis. These were sports that society at that time found socially acceptable.

But a few women during this time period had other ideas. Not only did these women try different sports than what most women were participating in at the time, but they also competed against men. Among the most notable women athletes in the early twentieth century are Madge Syers, Jackie Mitchell, and Babe Didrikson Zaharias.

MADGE SYERS (1881–1917)

In 1902, the rules did not even bother to exclude women from competing in the World Skating Championships because the idea that a woman would compete was so improbable. That is, until Florence Madeline Cave Syers came along. Born September 16, 1881, "Madge" Cave was one of fifteen children. Born into a wealthy London family, she excelled at swimming, horseback riding, and skating.

Madge Syers competed at the 1908 Olympic Games in London, winning the gold in the compulsory figures.

In 1899, Madge met Edgar Syers, who was eighteen years her senior. They quickly fell in love and became skating partners. Through their relationship, he challenged her to change her skating style. She soon discarded her stiff British skating technique and replaced it with a more fluid European approach. By 1900, the new couple had finished second in an international pairs event.

Following Edgar's encouragement, Madge entered the all-male 1902 World Championships. Everyone was shocked when she finished second to Sweden's Ulrich Salchow (the famous Salchow jump is named after him). This performance earned her a silver medal. Historians state that Ulrich was so impressed with Syers that he offered her his gold medal.

Not long after her performance, the International Skating Union barred women from its competitions. It cited three reasons. The first was "the difficulty of judging the feet of a competitor in a dress." The second was "the potential of a judge becoming attracted or attached to a participant," and the third was "the impossibility of comparing men to women."[1] Skating authorities in Great Britain had no problem with women competing against men. As a result, in 1903 Syers won the first British singles championship. She also defended her title the following year, when she defeated her husband.

Figure skating made its debut in the Olympics in 1908, and Syers won the gold medal in ladies' singles. Meanwhile, she and Edgar won a bronze in the pairs competition. Not long after, Syers became ill and was forced to retire. She died in 1917 at age thirty-five. Following her death, Edgar never skated again.

GERTRUDE EDERLE (1905–2003)

In 1926, American Gertrude Ederle became the first woman to swim across the English Channel. What's more, her time was faster than the five men who had done it before her. Born in New York City on October 23, 1905, Gertrude Ederle, better known as "Trudy," was already an Olympic gold medalist and was prepared to take on the channel at the age of nineteen. Unlike the men before her who used the breaststroke to cross the 21 miles (33.7 km) between France and England, she intended to do the crawl.

This swim was her second attempt. The first time, she was forced to get out of the water against her will. This time, she was prepared. Her older sister, Margaret, had designed a two-piece suit to keep her warm. Ederle also covered her body in sheep grease to stay warm and to protect her from jellyfish. Meanwhile, she kept her goggles in place with candle wax.

Historians note that Ederle started out her swim singing "Let Me Call You Sweetheart," to herself to set her pace. It wasn't long, though, before her trainer, Thomas Burgess, advised her to save her breath. During her twelfth hour at sea, the winds began to worry Burgess. He shouted at Ederle to come out of the water, but she refused. Once she saw the campfires along the English coast, there was no stopping her.

"When I walked out of the water, I began thinking, 'Oh my God, have I really done it?' When my feet hit the sand, oh, that was a wonderful moment," Ederle said.[2] What's more, a British passport official approached and jokingly asked for her papers.

Some estimate that the winds forced her to swim 14 extra miles (22.5 km). Still, her time of 14:31 was two hours better than the standing best. Once she returned to New York, Ederle was given a ticker tape parade. It was the biggest in history. What's more, Irving Berlin wrote a song for her, and President Calvin Coolidge invited her to the White House.

Later in life, doctors discovered that Ederle's hearing was damaged by all her time in the water. She also experienced a mental breakdown and a spinal injury that left her in constant pain.

But rather than give up, Ederle made the most of her situation. In a 1959 issue of *Sports Illustrated*, there is a photo of her teaching children at New York's Lexington School for the Deaf how to swim.

"They feel I'm one of them," she said, "and they trust me." Ederle lived a long life and impacted many young people. In 2003, she died in a New Jersey nursing home at the age of 98.[3]

JACKIE MITCHELL (1913–1987)

Jackie Mitchell, who was born in Chattanooga, Tennessee, on August 29, 1913, was a left-handed pitcher with a wicked curveball. Growing up, she lived next to future baseball Hall of Famer Dazzy Vance. Vance was a star pitcher for the Brooklyn Robins who helped Mitchell go on to make a name for herself. Apparently, Vance taught the

Had she been a man, Jackie Mitchell would have been a professional baseball star. Unfortunately, she was relegated to exhibition games and the women's league, despite being championed by Lou Gehrig (left) and Babe Ruth (right).

left-hander his favorite pitch, a curveball that could confuse even the best of batters.

Mitchell continued to perfect her pitching skills and eventually played for a women's team in Tennessee. She also attended a baseball school in Atlanta. During that time, she caught the attention of Joe Engel, a former major league pitcher who ran the Chattanooga Lookouts.

The *Chattanooga News* described Mitchell as a pitcher who "uses an odd, side-armed delivery, and puts both speed and curve on the ball. Her greatest asset, however, is control. She can place the ball where she pleases, and her knack at guessing the weakness of a batter is uncanny." The story also reported that Mitchell "believes that with careful training, she may soon be the first woman to pitch in the big leagues."[4]

In March 1931, her prediction came true. Engel offered seventeen-year-old Mitchell a contract. He was thinking ahead to an upcoming exhibition game against the New York Yankees and planned to showcase Mitchell's talents then. The game with the Yankees was scheduled for April Fool's Day, but rain forced the teams to postpone.

On April 2, in front of a crowd of four thousand people, Mitchell entered the game. She faced none other than Babe Ruth. According to historians, Mitchell threw a high ball on her first pitch. Then, Ruth swung and missed her next two pitches. He let the fourth pitch go by. But the umpire called it a strike, saying it crossed the corner of the plate. Ruth reportedly stomped back to his dugout in frustration and anger.

Lou Gehrig was the next batter. He swung and missed three straight pitches. After a standing ovation, Mitchell threw four balls and walked Tony Lazzeri. After that she was relieved by another pitcher. The *New York Times* later reported, "Perhaps Miss Jackie hasn't quite enough on the ball yet to bewilder Ruth and Gehrig in a serious game. But there are no such sluggers in the Southern Association, and she may win laurels this season, which cannot be ascribed to mere gallantry. The prospect grows gloomier for misogynists."[5]

Unfortunately, Jackie Mitchell never got the opportunity to see what else she could do. Baseball commissioner Kenesaw Mountain Landis voided her contract. He also said women were unfit for the game of baseball. Eventually, Mitchell retired from baseball and went to work for her father, an optometrist.[6] She died in January 1987 at seventy-four years old.

BABE DIDRIKSON ZAHARIAS (1911–1956)

Babe Didrikson Zaharias is arguably the greatest female athlete ever. Born Mildred Ella Didrikson on June 26, 1911, in Port Arthur, Texas, Babe earned her nickname

Many consider Babe Didrikson the greatest female athlete ever. This is particularly astonishing given the era in which she lived.

from her family, who called her "Baby" from the day she was born. After hitting a number of home runs in a baseball game when she was a teen, "Baby" was later shortened to "Babe."

Didrikson regularly played against men in basketball, baseball, and golf. In fact, she met her husband, wrestler George Zaharias, when they were paired together at the 1938 Los Angeles Open, a Professional Golfers' Association (PGA) tournament. Historians say he complained at first because he did not want to compete against a woman, but Babe must have won him over. They were married eleven months later.

As an athlete, Didrikson's accomplishments were many. She helped her Amateur Athletic Union (AAU) basketball team win the 1931 national championship. She also won gold medals in the javelin and 80-meter hurdles and took silver in the high jump at the 1932 Summer Olympics. But perhaps most noteworthy is the fact that she stayed at the top of women's golf for almost twenty years.

She also enjoyed success against men in golf. One account describes Didrikson's golf matchup with Grantland Rice and some of his colleagues at L.A.'s Brentwood Country Club. Paul Gallico was among the group. According to Don Van Natta, author of the Didrikson biography *Wonder Girl*, she wowed both men with her long drives and her precise short game.

Historians say that on the seventeenth hole, Didrikson challenged Gallico to a sprint from the tee to the green. Despite wearing a long dress, Didrikson's easily outran Gallico, who collapsed behind her. The race shook him up so much that he had to put four times on the hole.

"She is the longest hitter women's golf has ever seen," Rice wrote. "If Miss Didrikson would take up golf seriously, there is no doubt in my mind ... she would be a world beater in no time."[7]

Babe Didrikson Zaharias died at the age of forty-five in Texas after fighting a long battle with colon cancer.

FANNY BLANKERS-KOEN (1918–2004)

Often called the "Flying Housewife," Fanny Blankers-Koen was a natural when it came to track and field. In fact, she set world records in seven events. She was also the first woman to win four gold medals at a single Olympics.

Born April 26, 1918, in the Netherlands, Fanny Koen was a Dutch national champion in the 800-meter run by 1935. The following year, at seventeen, she placed sixth in the high jump and competed in the 4 x 100-meter relay at the Olympics in Berlin. In 1938, her time of 11 seconds in the 100-yard dash tied a world record. And in 1942 and 1943 she set records in the 80-meter hurdles, high jump, and long jump.[8]

Overall, Blankers-Koen set sixteen world records at eight different events, including 100-yard dash, 100-meter dash, 200-meter dash, high hurdles, high jump, long jump, pentathlon, and the 4 x 110-yard relay. She also won five European titles between 1946 and 1950 along with fifty-eight national championships in the Netherlands.[9]

Blankers-Koen faced considerable criticism as a woman athlete. Many believed she was too old to find success at the 1948 Olympics in London. Perhaps worse, she came under fire for pursuing her Olympic dreams as a wife and mother—as if she could not do both. That year, she easily won the 100-meter sprint. Meanwhile, she got off to a slow start in the 80-meter hurdles and bumped hurdle. As a result, this slowed her down and she won by only a small distance. When it came time for the 200-meter race, Blankers-Koen wanted to pull out of the race.

The pressure to win combined with the criticism she received for even participating made her second-guess her choice. She later had a change of heart and won the race decisively. In her last event of the games, the 4 x 100-meter relay, she put forward another great effort. After receiving the baton in fourth place, Blankers-Koen caught the lead runner at the finish line and led her team to victory.

In 1951, after the pentathlon was modified to include the shot put, high jump, 200-meter sprint,

80-meter hurdles, and long jump, Blankers-Koen set the first modern pentathlon record with 4,692 points. In her final Olympics in 1952, Blankers-Koen failed to win a medal. In 1999, the International Amateur Athletic Federation (IAAF) named Blankers-Koen the top female athlete of the twentieth century.[10]

Prior to her death in 2004 at the age of eighty-five, Fanny suffered from Alzheimer's disease. She was also somewhat deaf. She lived her final years in a psychiatric nursing home.

ALICE COACHMAN (1923–2014)

Born in Albany, Georgia, on November 9, 1923, Alice Coachman grew up in the segregated South. As a result, she was barred from public sports facilities because she was African American, so Coachman used whatever she could piece together to practice jumping. Dealing with the restrictions placed on her because of her race and the pressure women faced when they participated in sports, Coachman struggled to improve. But she persisted.

Track and field champion Alice Coachman was the first African American woman to win an Olympic gold medal.

In 1938, Coachman joined her high school track team. The boys' track coach noticed her talent and offered to work with her. As she continued to improve, Coachman was recognized by Tuskegee Institute in Alabama. In 1939, she enrolled in its high school program. Before she had even begun classes, she won the high jump competition in her first AAU national championship.

During the 1940s, Coachman collected a number of national titles. For instance, she won the AAU nationals in the high jump and the 50-meter dash while a senior. She also won national championships in the 50-meter dash, the 100-meter dash, the 4 x 100-meter relay, and the high jump.

Meanwhile, Coachman also competed on the women's basketball team, winner of three championships. She was named to five All-American teams and was the only African American on any of her teams.

Coachman missed out on the Olympic Games in 1940 and 1944 because World War II forced their cancellation. The games would have occurred during her college career. When Coachman finally did get the chance to compete in the 1948 Olympics in London, she had a back injury. But she still qualified and went on to set a record of 5 feet 6 1/8 inches. That year, she was the first African American woman to win an Olympic gold medal. She received her medal directly from King George VI himself.

Upon returning to the United States, Coachman was honored with a motorcade from Atlanta to Albany. And even though the ceremony was held in her honor, it was still segregated. Coachman retired shortly after her victory at the age of twenty-five.

Later, she formed the Alice Coachman Track and Field Foundation, which helps young athletes and former Olympians adjust to life after the games. In 1996, she was honored as one of the one hundred greatest Olympic athletes in history; and in 2004 she was inducted into the US Olympic Hall of Fame.[11]

Coachman died in July 2014 in Georgia. She was ninety years old and had been admitted to a nursing home after suffering a stroke.

OTHER NOTABLE FEMALE ATHLETES FROM THE EARLY 1900s

The first half of the twentieth century saw remarkable accomplishments from several other women athletes. Here are a few.

MAY KAARLUS

Billiards was mostly viewed as a male pastime in the late 1800s and early 1900s. However, Mary "May" Kaarlus is considered the first woman to specialize in trick shots. In 1901 while in New York City, she performed numerous billiards trick shots that many male players could not do. After that, the sixteen-year-old ambidextrous player soon became a billiards sensation. This was quite an accomplishment because women were barred from using a regular cue.

LULA OLIVE GILL

Lula Gill was the first female jockey to win a horse race in California. In 1906, when she competed, not many women were jockeys. Not long after Gill's win, Ada Evans Dean rode to victory when her horse's original jockey became ill. In fact, Dean won twice despite never having raced before.

ELEANORA SEARS

Eleanora Sears was the great-great-granddaughter of Thomas Jefferson and an all-around athlete. She is best known for her abilities in women's tennis and women's squash. But she also surprised her high-society friends and neighbors when she excelled at sports considered just for men. She played in trousers on a men's polo team and skippered a yacht that went on to beat Alfred Vanderbilt's yacht. She also raced speedboats and played football.

CONCHITA CINTRÓN

Given the danger involved, bullfighting has long been considered a man's sport. However, in 1937 Conchita Cintrón began bullfighting when she was just thirteen. During her thirteen years of bull fighting she eliminated eight hundred bulls. She did as well as any man and better than some. Cintrón is considered the first woman to compete as a professional bullfighter.[12]

FANNIE SPERRY STEELE

Fannie Sperry Steele was one of the first women inducted into the Rodeo Hall of Fame. As an award-winning bronco rider and rodeo performer, she was also the first Montana native in the National Cowgirl Hall of Fame. Steele also won several awards for her riding skills. For instance, she was named the Women's Bucking Horse Champion in 1904 at the age of seventeen. In both 1912 and 1913, she was the Lady Bucking Horse Champion of the World at the first Calgary Stampede. Hundreds of cowboys from western Canada, the United States, and Mexico competed.[13]

CHAPTER FIVE

BRINGING ABOUT CHANGE FROM THE 1950s TO THE 1970s

There was a time when many colleges and universities did not admit women. They also did not offer women athletic scholarships, and girls continued to face discrimination and ridicule when it came to sports. They were told that playing sports was not feminine. Women who were athletes were described as unattractive and selfish. Yet, women continued to defy barriers and suffer through ridicule because they loved to compete. It was in their blood, and they just wanted to play.

For instance, athlete Marge Snyder remembers, "I played on my Illinois high school's first varsity tennis team from 1968 to 1970. We were 56–0 over my three years. We were permitted to compete as long as we made no efforts to publicize our accomplishments and personally paid for our uniforms and equipment."[1]

But Title IX soon changed all of that. Title IX is a law passed by the US government to level the playing field for females both academically and athletically. It states that:

> No person in the United States shall, on the basis of sex, be excluded from participation in, be denied the benefits of, or be subjected to discrimination under any education program or activity receiving Federal financial assistance.

Title IX provided opportunities for women and girls when it came to sports as well as changed the way schools handled girls' sports. Under this law "institutions could not discriminate on the basis of gender, in any program receiving federal funds, including athletics."[2]

A CLOSER LOOK AT TITLE IX

Most people think Title IX applies only to sports, but the law also addresses nine additional areas. The other areas include access to higher education, career education, education for pregnant and parenting students, employment, learning environment, math and science, sexual harassment, standardized testing, and technology.

In the 1960s, women were fighting for equal rights and equal opportunities in education and employment. Leading the charge was Patsy Mink, a congresswoman from Hawaii. She was determined to change society's attitudes toward women. She was also the first woman of color to be elected to Congress. So she had experienced first-hand both race discrimination and sex discrimination. For instance, when she wanted to attend medical school, twenty different institutions turned her down. As a result, she went to law school. But following graduation, no law firm would hire her. Mink decided that she would enter politics to fight for gender and racial equality.

In 1972, Title IX was introduced by Patsy Mink and Edith Green. Another politician, Daniel Patrick Moynihan, later said that Title IX was one of the most important pieces of education legislation in history.

Unfortunately though, the passage of the bill got very little attention at first until Billie Jean King appeared on the scene. King, who could not get a tennis scholarship when she was a student Cal State Los Angeles, campaigned for higher pay and professional treatment for women tennis players. But it was her 1973 match against Bobby Riggs that put the ball in motion.

"I just had to play," King said in a later interview with *Newsweek*. "Title IX had just passed, and I ... wanted to change the hearts and minds of people to match the legislation."[3]

Things began to change quickly after that. By 1973, one year after Title IX was passed, there were college scholarships at the larger schools. There was also money set aside for equipment and uniforms. Plus girls' travel schedules were expanded. The impact the legislation has had has been astounding.

In 1971, less than 295,000 girls participated in high school varsity athletics. This number represented only 7 percent of all varsity athletes. By 2001, that number leaped to 2.8 million. Today, girls represent 41.5 percent of all varsity athletes, according to the National Coalition for Women and Girls in Education.

At the college level only 16,000 females competed in intercollegiate athletics in 1966. But by 2001, that number climbed to more than 150,000. What this means is that by 2001, 43 percent of all college athletes were female. What's more, a 2008 study of intercollegiate athletics showed that women's collegiate sports had grown to 9,101 teams, or 8.65 teams per school.[4]

ALTHEA GIBSON (1927–2003)

Before Billie Jean King came along, Althea Gibson was blazing trails of her own in tennis, especially for African American women. Gibson was the first black player to play international tennis; and in 1956 she became the first person of color, man or

Althea Gibson's hard work and refusal to give up paid off when she became the first African American player to compete at Wimbledon.

woman, to win a Grand Slam title when she won the French Open.

Throughout her career, she won eleven Grand Slam titles and was inducted into the International Tennis Hall of Fame. She also had a professional golf career.[5]

Althea Gibson was born on August 25, 1927, in South Carolina. Her parents were sharecroppers who left their rural farm in 1930 and headed to New York City. Raised primarily in Harlem, Althea's life was hard. She grew up on public assistance, but she loved sports and spent a lot of time competing. When she won several tournaments hosted by the local recreation department, Gibson started getting the attention of others. In 1941, she started playing on the Harlem River Tennis Courts.

Remarkably, Gibson won a local tournament sponsored by the American Tennis Association (ATA) after she had only been playing for one year. The ATA was an organization established to promote and sponsor tournaments for black players. She won more ATA titles in 1944 and

1945. Gibson won ten straight championships from 1947 to 1956.

Gibson attended college on an athletic scholarship and graduated in 1953. Several times throughout her career, she almost gave up tennis because so much was closed off to her. In the Unites States, the sport was not only dominated by whites, but it was also segregated.

In 1950, Alice Mable, a former number one player herself, wrote a commentary in *American Lawn Tennis* magazine blasting the tennis community for not allowing a player like Althea Gibson to compete in the world's best tournaments. By 1951, Gibson was invited to Wimbledon and became the first African American ever to play in the tournament. A year later, she was a top ten player in the United States.

In 1955, Gibson traveled around the world on a sponsorship from the US State Department. She competed in places like India, Pakistan, and Burma. By 1956, all the pieces seemed to fall into place for Gibson when she won the French Open. She followed up with the Wimbledon and US Open titles in 1957 and 1958.

When it was all said and done, Althea Gibson won fifty-six singles and doubles championships before turning pro in 1959. Following her retirement, she was inducted into the International Tennis Hall of Fame in 1971. And in 1975, she served ten years as commissioner of athletics in New Jersey. She was also a member of the governor's council on physical fitness.[6] Althea Gibson died in New Jersey in September 2003 at the age of seventy-six.

BILLIE JEAN KING (1943–)

One of the most instrumental women in the advancement of female rights in athletics was tennis star Billie Jean King. Her advocacy for women's sports in the 1960s and 1970s transformed sports at every level. King also helped make it more acceptable for girls and women to be athletes. In fact, in the 1975 issue of *Seventeen*, a readers' poll discovered that Billie Jean King was the most admired woman in the world.[7]

Billie Jean King's accomplishments off the court have been even more remarkable than her impressive career.

What's more, she is one of the most admired tennis players in history. King was born Billie Jean Moffit on November 22, 1943, in Long Beach, California. She began playing tennis at eleven years old. After one of her first tennis lessons, historians note that she told her mother, "I'm going to be number one in the world."[8] And she was. She was the number one tennis player five times between 1966 and 1972.

Billie Jean King dominated the tennis world for more than twenty years. She won thirty-nine Grand Slam singles, doubles, and mixed doubles tennis titles. These titles included a record twenty titles at Wimbledon.

Throughout her career, King fought for equal prize money and equal treatment of women. She also helped establish the Virginia Slims Tour and founded both the Women's Tennis Association and the Women's Sports Foundation. She also cofounded World Team Tennis.

King is credited with a slew of milestones. For instance, in 1971, she became the first female athlete in any sport to earn more than $100,000 in a single season. In 1974, leading the Philadelphia Freedoms, she became the first woman to coach a co-ed team in professional sports. And in 1984, King became the first female commissioner in professional sports history. She was awarded the Presidential Medal of Freedom, the nation's highest civilian honor, in 2009.[9]

It was her match against tennis great Bobby Riggs that people most remember. On September 20, 1973, Bobby Riggs, a Wimbledon champion and a top-ranked tennis player through the late 1940s, played against Billie Jean King. In this "Battle of the Sexes," King was seen as playing for the honor of all women.

"I thought it would set us back 50 years if I didn't win that match," King later said. "It would ruin the women's tour and affect all women's self-esteem."[10]

At twenty-nine, King had already won five Wimbledon and three US Open singles titles. But nothing she did had as much impact as her match with fifty-five-year-old Riggs. Riggs had recently beaten her rival Margaret Court, 6–2, 6–1, in an exhibition match, so there was a lot on the line.[11] In fact, Riggs reportedly said, "the best way to handle women is to keep them pregnant and barefoot."[12]

After months of promotion, the day of the match arrived amid a great deal of fanfare. Before the match began, both players gave the other symbolic gifts. Riggs presented King with a giant lollipop while she handed him a piglet, a symbol of male chauvinism. By the end of the day though, King had emerged the victor. She defeated Riggs in three straight sets, 6–4, 6–3, 6–3.

Although the event was strictly for publicity, it became arguably the most famous tennis match in history. What's more, it became a symbol of women's equality, coming during the early years of the new women's movement.

Billie Jean King's solid victory significantly boosted the credibility of women's participation in major sports. Coming on the heels of Title IX, the match confirmed that women do have a place in sports. Long-held beliefs and stereotypes were finally breaking down.[13]

DONNA DE VARONA (1947–)

At just thirteen years old, Donna de Varona was the youngest competitor at the 1960 Olympic Games. Over the next four years, she broke eighteen world swimming records and won two Olympic gold medals. By the time she was seventeen, she was voted Most Outstanding Female Athlete in the world by both the Associated Press and the United Press International.

With thirty-seven national championships and two Olympic gold medals under her belt, de Varona retired from competitive sports in 1965. That same year, she became the first female sports broadcaster on network television. This accomplishment opened doors for future female athletes and journalists.

Born April 26, 1947, in San Diego, California, de Varona earned recognition for both her swimming and her sports journalism. For instance, she earned an Emmy Award nomination for *Keepers of the Flame*, a television special about the Olympics. She also received an Emmy for her story about a Special Olympian. What's more, she won the Gracie Award two years in a row for her Sporting News Radio show, *Donna de Varona on Sports.*

De Varona is one of the founding members of the Women's Sports Foundation and its first president. She also served five terms on the President's Council on Physical Fitness and Sports and played a key part in the passage of the 1978 Amateur Sports Act and the 1972 landmark Title IX legislation.

De Varona's other honors include the International Swimming Hall of Fame Gold Medallion and the Olympia Award for her contribution to the Olympic Movement. She also received the Olympic Order. This award is the highest given by the IOC.[14]

WILMA RUDOLPH (1940–1994)

On June 23, 1940, Wilma Rudolph was born prematurely, weighing just 4.5 pounds (2 kilograms). As a result, the family's doctor doubted she would live. But she did. Still, she developed pneumonia and polio. These conditions disabled her for most of her childhood. For several years, her mother, brother, or sister massaged her legs four times a day. She also wore a metal brace for several years and did not start school until she was eight.[15]

But Wilma was a fighter. She defied all odds when she became a track and field star. Initially, Wilma did not make the eighth grade track team,

The fastest woman of the 1960s, Wilma Rudolph won Olympic medals at Melbourne and Rome. She became the first American woman to win three gold medals at a single Olympics in 1960.

but her sister did. Wilma's father told the track coach that the Rudolph sisters were a "package deal." Either both girls made the team, or neither of the girls made the team.

As a result, Wilma was put on the team. She also played basketball. Her coaches soon gave her the nickname "Skeeter" because she buzzed around them during games, hoping to get put in.

A few years later, when Rudolph participated in a track meet at Tuskegee Institute she lost every single race. But the track coach of Tennessee State University (TSU) thought she had potential and recruited her. She participated in his summer track camps at TSU. A year later, when she was just sixteen, Rudolph won a bronze medal at the 1956 Olympics.[16]

By the time she was seventeen, Rudolph was pregnant. Once she had the baby, she did not participate in sports. She sat out her senior year during track season. For a while it looked like she might never participate in track again. But the next year her sister took care of her baby girl so she could attend TSU. As a member of the track team there, Rudolph devoted herself to running and earned a place on the 1960 Olympic team.[17]

At the Olympics that year, Rudolph became the first American woman to win three gold medals in track and field. Her events included the 100 meters, 200 meters, and 4 x 100-meter relay. These accomplishments made her a star in the United

States and abroad. As a result, Rudolph was named the Associated Press's female athlete of the year in 1960 and 1961.

Although Rudolph retired in 1962 at the age of twenty-two, she remained a pioneer for both civil rights and women's rights.[18] She went on to become a schoolteacher and an athletic coach. Then for more than two decades, she worked to teach others what she had learned about amateur athletics. Wilma Rudolph died from brain cancer in Tennessee in November 1994.

KATHRINE SWITZER (1947–)

In 1967, Kathrine Switzer became the first woman to run the Boston Marathon with an official race number. She accomplished this feat despite the best efforts of race director Jock Semple. He tried to forcibly remove her from the course. Photos of him running at her were in newspapers around the world.

Switzer was born in Amberg, Germany, on January 5, 1947. But two years later, she moved to the United States. She grew up in Virginia playing field hockey and basketball. She also ran a mile each day.

Switzer attended Lynchburg College and competed in track and field. There were only a few short-distance events available to women at the time. By 1966, she transferred to Syracuse University. While there, she began training with the

It is shocking to think that only half a century ago, women were discouraged from running the famed Boston Marathon. In 1967, the marathon organizer attempted to physically push runner Katherine Switzer off the course.

men's cross-country team. During this time, Switzer decided to run the Boston Marathon. There was nothing in the official rulebook prohibiting women from running. What's more, she signed up for the race and used the name "K. V. Switzer." She used this name to sign all of her work. So it made sense to register for the race with the same name. She was not intentionally trying to hide her identity.

She also had no intention of making a political statement. She just loved running and wanted to be able to say she finished a famous race. About roughly four miles in, Jock Semple had different plans.

"Get the hell out of my race and give me those numbers!" he shouted as he attempted to snatch the numbers from her chest. But her boyfriend, Tom Miller, blocked him. Although nervous and upset, Switzer managed to finish the race. Following the incident, Switzer was inspired to help other female athletes accomplish their goals. She felt no woman should be denied the opportunity to participate in the sports she loved. What's more, she continued running.

In 1974, Switzer won the New York City Marathon. She also placed second at the Boston Marathon, which had finally begun accepting female runners in 1972. She ran that race in 2:51:37, her personal best.

In 1977, Switzer created the Avon International Running Circuit, a worldwide series of women's races. This organization was instrumental in helping the women's marathon become an Olympic event. During the first Olympic marathon, Switzer provided commentary for the ABC telecast.[19]

NADIA COMANECI (1961–)

At the tender age of fourteen, Nadia Comaneci became the first woman to score a perfect 10 in an Olympic gymnastics event. Born on November 12, 1961, in Romania, Nadia was discovered at the age of six by now-legendary gymnastics coach Béla Károlyi. She won the Romanian National Junior Championships, and, as a senior, won the European Championships in 1975 and the American Cup in 1976.

At the 1976 Olympic Games in Montreal, Comaneci received seven perfect scores and won three gold medals, for the uneven bars, balance beam, and individual all-around. She also won a bronze medal as part of the Romanian national team. Comaneci's performance at the 1976 Olympics was so flawless that it set the expectations of future athletes in the sport. Viewers and judges would no longer be content with what they had seen in the past from gymnasts.

At the 1980 Olympic Games, Comaneci won two gold medals, for the balance beam and floor exercise, and two silver medals, for the team competition and individual all-around.

Comaneci retired from gymnastics in 1984. She was a coach for the Romanian team, but in 1989, she defected to the United States via Hungary. In 1999, she received a World Sports Award of the

Romanian gymnast Nadia Comaneci scored the Olympics' first perfect 10 at the age of fourteen. The decorated gymast is still involved in the sport.

Century after being elected Athlete of the Century during a gala in Vienna, Austria.[20] Today, she is active in many charities and international organizations. She sometimes provides commentary for gymnastic meets.

JANET GUTHRIE (1938–)

Janet Guthrie enjoyed going fast and taking risks. For this reason, she fell in love with auto racing. And in 1977, she became the first woman to qualify for the Indianapolis 500. She finished twelfth that year. Born on March 7, 1938, in Iowa City, Guthrie was the daughter of a Miami-based airline pilot. At seventeen, she got her own pilot's license. Historians say she challenged her boyfriend at the time to see who could fly higher.

Guthrie graduated from the University of Michigan in 1960 with a degree in physics. Her goal was to pursue a career in aeronautical engineering. She even applied to NASA's first scientist-astronaut program and made the first cut. But her pursuit of this goal did not last long.

When Guthrie bought a Jaguar XK 120 coupe, she started competing in street races. By 1972, she decided to compete in auto racing full-time. She first made a name for herself at the 12 Hours of Sebring, and by 1976, Indy team owner Rolla Vollstedt expressed interest in taking her on as a driver. He wanted a female driver that would bring attention to his team.

In 1977, she qualified at Indy in a Vollstedt car. But mechanical troubles set in after only sixteen laps. In that race, she finished twenty-ninth and a significant distance behind the winner, A. J. Foyt. The next year, Guthrie formed her own team and secured Texaco Star as the primary sponsor. She started fifteenth and finished ninth in the race, ahead of famous Indy drivers Mario Andretti, Johnny Rutherford, and Rick Mears. Even more amazing, she finished the race with a broken wrist. She had injured it a few days earlier in a tennis match but did not let the pain keep her from racing.

Guthrie's last major race was the 1980 Daytona 500. She finished in eleventh place. "I didn't retire," she is noted as saying. "I ran out of money."[21]

CHAPTER SIX

LEVELING THE PLAYING FIELD: FROM THE 1980s TO THE 1990s

W omen's sports expanded at an astonishing rate after Title IX was passed. For example, in 1964 women participated in only six sports in the summer Olympics, and by 1984 women participated in sixteen sports. One of the most notable additions that year was the women's marathon, which had never been part of the Olympic Games before.

Another example of the significant expansion of women's sports included intercollegiate championships and athletic scholarships. None of those existed in 1966, but in 1981 four national organizations offered intercollegiate tournaments or championships for women. Additionally, more than eight hundred colleges and universities provided women with athletic scholarships.[1]

Although there was still much to be done regarding equality and opportunity, the road to participate in sports seemed clear for women in the 1980s and 1990s. As a result, more women and girls began pursuing their athletic dreams. There were some bumps in the road along the way and there were still a number of firsts to be accomplished, but things were looking more optimistic for the female athlete.

PAT SUMMITT (1952–2016)

Pat Summitt was named the head coach at Tennessee in 1974, when women's college basketball was yet to be recognized by the National Collegiate Athletic Association (NCAA). Under her leadership, the Tennessee Lady Volunteers (better known as the Vols) won their first national championship in 1987. They went on to win seven more national titles before her retirement. They also won thirty-two Southeastern Conference (SEC) championships.

Seven times she was named NCAA Coach of the Year and was inducted into six halls of fame. Summitt retired from coaching in 2012 due to early-onset Alzheimer's. During her thirty-eight-year career, she achieved 1,098 career victories, which is more than any male or female coach in NCAA history.[2]

"I remind people that I've never scored a basket for the University of Tennessee," she told the *New York Times* as she approached her one-thousandth victory.[3]

Thanks in great part to the achievements of Pat Summitt, women's basketball has gained tremendous popularity and respect. The seven-time NCAA Coach of the Year inspired athletes and casual fans alike.

Summitt was born Patricia Head on June 14, 1952, in Clarksville, Tennessee. When she was in high school, her family moved to Henrietta, Tennessee, because the school she had been attending did not have a girl's basketball team. She excelled in basketball and later played in college, but her parents paid her way because there were no scholarships for women at the time. Meanwhile, her brothers attended college on basketball scholarships.

Summitt was a cocaptain on the United States

National Women's Basketball Team in the 1976 Olympics. She and her team won a silver medal that year. Eight years later, she coached the US women's team to a gold medal.

Throughout her college coaching career, Summitt helped create excitement around women's basketball. It quickly became more than just a club sport. Women's basketball is now one of the most popular sports in America.

What's more, Summitt's passion for the sport inspired others as well. For instance, seventy-four former Lady Vols players, assistants, and graduate assistants followed in her footsteps and became coaches. Seventeen are currently college head coaches.

Summitt was also recognized in areas outside of basketball. In 1997, she was honored by *Working Mother* magazine at the White House and named one of the 25 Most Influential Working Mothers. In 2007, *U.S. News & World Report* named her one of America's Best Leaders; and in 2012 she received the Presidential Medal of Freedom.

Summitt succumbed to Alzheimer's disease on June 28, 2016.[4]

JOAN BENOIT (1957–)

Joan Benoit qualified for the first-ever Olympic marathon in 1984 just seventeen days after arthroscopic knee surgery. She went on to win the gold in that event.

Born on May 16, 1957, Benoit started running when she was fifteen. She had broken a leg skiing and used running to recover from surgery. In high school, Benoit had a lot of success competing with her track team. She continued competing in college. Because of Title IX, Benoit had more opportunities for college sports than other runners before her had.

In 1979, while still in college, Benoit entered the Boston Marathon. On her way to the race, she got caught in traffic and was going to miss the start. So she ran two miles before the race began just to make it to the starting point. Her late arrival also forced her to start at the back of the pack. Yet she quickly pulled ahead and won the marathon, with a time of 2:35:15, despite her extra running in the beginning.

In December 1981, Benoit was suffering from recurring heel pain. So, she had surgery on both Achilles tendons. Despite the pain and the surgeries, Benoit did not let it hold her back. The following September, she won a New England marathon with a time of 2:26:11. This time was a new record for women and two minutes faster than the previous record.

In April 1983, she entered the Boston Marathon, again prepared to face a new world record time. Grete Waitz, a rival of Benoit's, had set a new world record in the women's marathon the day before with a time of 2:25:29. Meanwhile, Allison Roe of New Zealand was expected to win the race. That day proved to be interesting. Roe dropped out of the race due to leg cramps. Meanwhile, Benoit beat Waitz's record by more than two minutes, with a time of 2:22:42. This time was good enough to qualify her for the Olympics.

Benoit began training for the Olympic trials, which would be held in May 1984. But in March, her knee started giving her problems. She tried both rest and an anti-inflammatory drug. But, neither attempt resolved the issue.

In April, she finally agreed to arthroscopic surgery on her right knee. Four days after surgery, she started running and training again, but she continued to have problems with her right knee as well as issues with her left hamstring. She again did not let the pain stop her and ran in the Olympic trials anyway. By mile seventeen, Benoit was leading the race. Historians note that she continued pushing herself even though her legs were tight and painful for the last miles. Amazingly, she finished first and qualified for the Olympics even though she had just had surgery weeks earlier. This race would be the first women's marathon in the Olympic Games.

Because the Olympics were scheduled for summer in Los Angeles, Benoit trained during the hottest part of the day. She expected the marathon to be very hot and wanted to be prepared. Everyone expected Grete Waitz to win gold that year considering all of Benoit's injuries. But Benoit had different plans. On the day of the race, Benoit took an early lead and no one could catch her. She finished the race with a time of 2:24:52. Her time was the third best for a women's marathon and the best in any all-women marathon. Waitz won the silver medal.[5]

JACKIE JOYNER-KERSEE (1962–)

Jackie Joyner was born on March 3, 1962, in East St. Louis, Illinois. Her parents, who were only teenagers at the time, named her Jacqueline after then-First Lady Jacqueline Kennedy. The family says that one of her grandmothers said the day she was born, "Some day this girl will be the first lady of something."[6]

Because she knew the challenges of being a teen mom, Jackie's mother encouraged her to focus on athletics instead of dating. As a result, Jackie developed an interest in track and field. Eventually, she enrolled in the new track program at the local Mary Brown Community Center. Her brother Al became her training partner.

Al remembered how much he and his sister wanted to rise above the conditions in which they lived. In the beginning, Jackie didn't win many

The early death of her mother gave Jackie Joyner-Kersee the drive to succeed in sports. Her record-breaking accomplishments in track and field surpassed all expectations.

races but after watching the 1976 Olympics, she became inspired.

Jackie excelled at Lincoln High School. Not only was she a state champion in both track and basketball, but she also graduated in the top 10 percent of her class. And beginning when she was fourteen, she won four straight national junior pentathlon championships. She also played volleyball in high school.

After graduating, Joyner attended the University of California, Los Angeles (UCLA) on a basketball scholarship. That same year, her mother died suddenly at thirty-seven from meningitis. Following her mother's funeral, Joyner put all of her energy into sports. She was determined to honor her mother's desire for her to succeed.

When she returned to college after her mother's death, Bob Kersee, an assistant track coach, offered her support both athletically and emotionally. Kersee saw Joyner's all-round athletic potential. He convinced her that multi-event track should be her sport instead of basketball. He was so convinced that he threatened to quit his job at the university if they did not allow her scholarship to switch from basketball to the heptathlon. The university agreed, and Kersee became her coach.

In 1984, Joyner won the Olympic silver medal in the heptathlon. In 1985, she set an American record in the long jump, at 23 feet 9 inches (7.45 m). In 1986, she married Bob Kersee and changed her name to Jackie Joyner-Kersee. She went on that year to set a new world record in the heptathlon at the Goodwill Games in Moscow, with 7,148 points, becoming the first woman to surpass 7,000 points.

She beat her own record just three weeks later, scoring 7,158 points in the US Olympic Festival in Houston, Texas. For these achievements, she received both the James E. Sullivan Award and the Jesse

Owens Award. Over the next fifteen years, Joyner-Kersee won many more events, titles, and awards.

She retired from track and field in 2001 and is the founder and chair of the Jackie Joyner-Kersee Foundation. The foundation was created to provide youth, adults, and families with the resources to improve their quality of life and to enhance communities worldwide.[7]

NANCY LIEBERMAN (1958–)

Nancy Lieberman's basketball journey began in Harlem, where she developed a reputation as a gritty basketball powerhouse. Born on July 1, 1958, in Brooklyn, New York, Nancy played pickup basketball games with boys but did not play on a girl's basketball team until her sophomore year of high school. Although Nancy's mother was not supportive of her interest in basketball, Nancy persevered. By 1975, she had secured one of twelve coveted spots on the USA Women's National Basketball Team.

This move made her a nationally-recognized name. A year later, she won a silver medal at the World Championships and a gold medal at the Pan American Games. At eighteen years old, she earned a silver medal at the 1976 Summer Olympics. She was the youngest basketball player, male or female, to medal at the Olympics.

While in college, Lieberman's recognition as a basketball great continued. For instance, she became the first-ever two-time winner of the prestigious Wade Trophy. The award recognizes the player of the year in women's college basketball. She was also selected as the Broderick Award Winner for Basketball. Additionally, she received three consecutive Kodak All-American honors.

In 1981, Lieberman became a professional basketball player. The Dallas Diamonds drafted her, and she quickly made her mark in the league. The Diamonds were part of the first Women's Professional Basketball League (WBL). By 1984, Lieberman was the league MVP and led her team to a championship.

After playing for the WBL, Lieberman turned to the men's league, becoming the only woman to play in a men's professional sports league. In 1986, she played with the Springfield Fame in the United States Basketball League (USBL). In 1987, she joined the Long Island Knights, also in the USBL. And in 1988, Lieberman toured with the Washington Generals. The Generals are opponents and rivals of the acclaimed Harlem Globetrotters.

When Lieberman was thirty-nine, she came out of retirement to play for the Phoenix Mercury. It was 1997, the inaugural season of the Women's National Basketball Association (WNBA).

Lieberman was the oldest player to ever play in the league. She retired again and was named general manager and head coach of the WNBA's Detroit Shock in 1998. She led the team to the highest winning percentage of any expansion team in professional sports. She was also runner-up for coach of the year.

Then on July 24, 2008, she returned to the WNBA for one game. She was fifty at the time and broke her own record as the oldest player to ever play in the league.

In 2009, she became the first-ever female head coach in the National Basketball Association (NBA). She accepted the head coaching position for the Texas Legends. They are the Dallas Mavericks' NBA D-League team. In their first season as an expansion team, she led them to the play-offs. When she became the assistant coach of the Sacramento Kings, she became the second female in history to coach in the NBA.[8]

MIA HAMM (1972–)

Born Mariel Margaret Hamm on March 17, 1972, in Selma, Alabama, Mia Hamm is considered the best female soccer player in history by most soccer enthusiasts. Although she was born with a clubfoot and had to wear corrective shoes as a toddler, she became an outstanding athlete.

Mia Hamm's long soccer career included many awards and championships. Perhaps more important, Hamm brought much-needed attention to the sport of women's soccer in the United States.

Mia was first introduced to soccer while her family was stationed on a US Air Force base in Italy. And she quickly became one of the sport's great players. For instance, at the age of fifteen, Hamm was the youngest soccer player to play for the national team. While at the University of North Carolina, she helped lead the team to four consecutive NCAA women's championships.

Overall, Hamm played with the US women's national soccer team for seventeen years. As a result, she has one of the largest fan bases of any American athlete. In 1991, when she was nineteen, she was the youngest team member in history to win the World Cup. Five years later, she and her teammates secured the gold medal at the 1996 Summer Olympics. They won gold again in 2004.

In 1999, Hamm set a new record for most international goals scored when she made her 108th goal for the US team. She held that title until June 2013. Her other accomplishments include being elected Soccer USA's Female Athlete of the Year five years in a row between 1994 and 1998. She was also named MVP of the Women's Cup in 1995.

Hamm has won three ESPY Awards, including awards as the Soccer Player of the Year and Female Athlete of the Year. In 2004, she and teammate Michelle Akers were named on the Fédération Internationale de Football Association's (FIFA) list of the 125 Greatest Living Soccer Players. Not only were they the only Americans to be named to the list, but they were also the only women.

In 1999, Hamm founded the Mia Hamm Foundation, an organization committed to bone marrow research. Hamm founded the group after her brother, Garrett, died of complications from a rare blood disease called aplastic anemia.[9]

VENUS WILLIAMS (1980–)

Venus Williams had a tough childhood growing up in Compton near Los Angeles, California. But with hard work and dedication she became a champion tennis player and four-time Olympic gold medalist. Born June 17, 1980, Venus, along with her sister, Serena, has transformed the tennis world. Their strength and athleticism have set the standard for other players to aim for.

Williams's father, Richard Williams, is the one who first introduced Venus and her sister to tennis. A former sharecropper from Louisiana, he scoured tennis books and videos looking for techniques to teach his girls. What's more, it was no accident that he moved his girls to Compton, where gang activity was high. Richard wanted to expose his daughters to what life could be like if they did not work hard and get an education.

As it turned out, the girls were phenomenal

tennis players, even at a young age. By the time she turned ten, Venus's serve was more than 100 miles (160 km) per hour. She used this advantage to go 63–0 on the United States Tennis Association junior tour. In 1997, she became the first unseeded US Open women's finalist in the open era. And, in 2000, she won both Wimbledon and the US Open. These accomplishments opened the door for a $40 million contract with Reebok. But she was more than a one-hit wonder. Venus went on to defend her titles in 2001.

At the 2000 Olympics, Venus took the gold medal in the singles competition, and then took a second gold in doubles with Serena. After that though, Venus had to limit her playing time due to a wrist injury. As a result, she competed in only a handful of tournaments. But by 2007, she returned with the same power she had previously and won Wimbledon. She repeated the victory a year later, when she defeated her sister Serena for a fifth career Wimbledon championship. A few months later, the two sisters captured the doubles title at the 2008 Olympics.

In 2011, Venus was diagnosed with Sjogren's syndrome. This syndrome is an autoimmune disease. It caused her to feel fatigued and sore much of the time. She did what she could to live with the condition and get healthier. For instance,

Sisters, doubles partners, and competitors Serena and Venus Williams changed the face of women's tennis. The sisters' power games have dominated the sport for nearly two decades.

she switched to a vegan diet. She also altered her training schedule to allow for more recovery days. These changes proved to be somewhat successful.

By 2012, she and Serena claimed their thirteenth Grand Slam doubles title at Wimbledon. That fall, Venus also won her first Women's Tennis Association (WTA) singles title in more than two years. And in early 2015, she claimed her forty-sixth career singles title at the ASB Classic.

Although her health continues to dog her, Venus has flashes of brilliance of her glory days. In 2016, she made it all the way to the semifinals at Wimbledon in singles play. In addition, she won a silver medal in mixed doubles at the Summer Olympics.

When she is not playing tennis, Venus has a number of different interests that keep her busy. She started a clothing line called EleVen. She also developed a collection of women's apparel for Wilson's Leather. She even has her own interior design company, V*Starr Interiors. In addition to her design interests, Venus has been involved with a number of social service organizations. She works with the United Nations Educational, Scientific and Cultural Organization (UNESCO) to promote gender equality around the world.

Venus and Serena also became the first African American women to buy shares of an NFL team. They joined the group of owners for the Miami Dolphins in 2009.[10]

SERENA WILLIAMS (1981–)

Born September 26, 1981, in Saginaw, Michigan, Serena Williams is the youngest of Richard and Oracene Williams's five daughters. At three, Serena practiced tennis two hours a day with her father. That early commitment to tennis paid off.

By 1991, Serena was ranked first in the ten-and-under division. She was also 46–3 on the junior United States Tennis Association tour. Although the girls spent a considerable amount of time in Compton, near Los Angeles, Richard eventually moved the family to Florida. He felt the girls needed better tennis instruction to become professionals and decided Florida was the place to make that happen. While there, Richard let go of some of his coaching responsibilities. However, at one point in their careers he scaled back their junior tournament schedule because he was concerned they would burn out.

In 1995, Serena turned pro. Three years later, she graduated from high school and almost immediately signed a $12 million shoe deal with Puma. In 1999, she beat out her sister Venus for the family's first Grand Slam win, when she captured the US Open title.

In 2002, Serena won the French Open, the US Open, and Wimbledon. Remarkably, it was Venus whom she defeated in the finals of each tournament.

She captured her first Australian Open in 2003. That victory made her one of only six women in the open era to complete a career Grand Slam. The win also fulfilled her desire to hold all four major titles simultaneously, which became known as the "Serena Slam." In 2008, she won the US Open and teamed up with Venus to capture a second women's doubles Olympic gold medal.

But like her sister, Serena also had her down times. She underwent knee surgery in August 2003. She was also devastated by the sudden death of one of her sisters. As a result, she was no longer motivated to stay in shape or to compete. Her tennis ranking dropped to 139.

But her faith in God as a Jehovah's Witness helped stabilize her. Then she took a life-changing trip to west Africa. As a result, she saw her competitiveness return. By 2009, she won both the Australian Open singles and Wimbledon. She also won the doubles matches at both the Australian Open and Wimbledon that year. In 2010, Serena won the Australian Open singles and doubles matches, as well as her fourth Wimbledon singles championship.

But in 2011, Serena suffered a series of health scares. Doctors found a blood clot in one of her lungs. She also underwent several other health procedures. And she had surgery to remove a hematoma.

But in 2012 she won her fifth Wimbledon singles title. She also won her first major championship in two years. And at the Olympics that year, she took her first gold in women's singles. The next day, she claimed her fourth overall Olympic gold when she played doubles with her sister Venus.

In 2013, Serena captured her second French Open title as well as her sixteenth Grand Slam singles title. Venus clinched her third straight and sixth overall US Open singles title in 2014. In 2015, she won the Australian Open. At the French Open that same year, Serena overcame an illness to win the tournament for the third time and claim her twentieth Grand Slam singles title.

That summer, Serena faced her big sister Venus. She had to get past her in order to advance past the fourth round at Wimbledon, and she did it. A few days later, she claimed her second career "Serena Slam." She also became the oldest Grand Slam singles champion in the open era.

It is difficult to keep up with Serena's accolades. Remarkably, she continues to compete at possibly the highest level of her career, even well past the age of retirement for most players. Off the court, Serena's passion involves helping underprivileged children around the world. She works tirelessly to provide educational opportunities to these young people. She has also formed the Serena Williams Foundation, which helps build schools in Africa.[11]

CHAPTER SEVEN

CARRYING THE TORCH FORWARD IN THE NEW MILLENNIUM

Title IX has changed everything. From the time that President Richard Nixon signed it into law in 1972 to the present, nine times as many girls play high school sports as before Title IX. Additionally, there has been a 450 percent increase of women in collegiate athletics.[1]

More girls play soccer today than all the girls who played youth sports in 1970. What's more, in that same year only one of every twenty-seven girls played high school varsity sports compared to one in three today. Overall, women now outnumber men as active sports and fitness participants.[2] And for the first time in history, women were represented in every Olympic competition in 2012.

Yet, inequalities still exist. According to the National Coalition for Women and Girls in Education, girls have "1.3 million fewer chances to play sports in high school than boys. And, less than two-thirds of African American and Hispanic girls play sports, while more than three-quarters of Caucasian girls do."[3]

As a result, women today still continue to push against the boundaries that restrain them. Here is a closer look at some of the female athletes that are making strides for women today.

TEGLA LOROUPE (1973–)

Born on May 9, 1973, Tegla Loroupe is a Kenyan long-distance runner who grew up with twenty-four siblings. As a child, she spent her time working in the fields and looking after her younger brothers and sisters. Yet she never complained. As a result, she was given the nickname "Chametia," which means "the one who never gets annoyed."

When Tegla started school at age seven, she would run all the way there. The catch was that the run was more than 10 kilometers (6.2 miles) in one direction and she did it while barefoot. This is where her talent for running was first noticed. But her father did not support her running aspirations. Only her mother and older sister supported her dream to become a runner. At one point, her father even banned her from running. He felt running was not ladylike. But Tegla persisted and kept running.

Even though her father insisted that women should not be runners, Tegla Loroupe kept running. In 1994, Loroupe became the first African woman to win the New York City Marathon.

Initially, the Kenyan athletics federation was not impressed with Loroupe. But in 1988, she won an important cross-country race and caught the federation's attention. By 1989, she was nominated for the junior world championships. There she finished twenty-eighth. After that, she continued to train full-time.

In 1994, Loroupe established herself as an important part of Africa's athletic community when she ran her first major marathon in New York City and won. This win made her the first African woman to win the New York City Marathon. It also elevated her as a role model for young women everywhere, especially in Kenya. What's more, Kenya finally had a female runner to showcase along with its talented male athletes.

Between 1997 and 1999, Loroupe won three consecutive world half-marathon championships. And in the World Championships, she won bronze in the 10,000 meters in both 1995 and 1999.

During the 2000 Olympics, Loroupe was expected to leave victorious. But the night before the race, she came down with food poisoning. Despite being sick, she still managed to finish the marathon. She placed thirteenth. Loroupe also ran the 10,000 meters and placed fifth. Loroupe later said that she ran the marathon despite being sick because she felt a sense of duty to everyone who looks up to her as a role model for Kenya.

What's more, Loroupe held the world record for the marathon between April 1998 and September 2001. She set her first world record in the 1998 Rotterdam Marathon with a time of 2:20:47. She later improved on that time in 1999 at the Berlin Marathon when she crossed the line at 2:20:43.

Despite the fact that Loroupe ran a variety of distance events, the marathon was her most successful running event. She won the Rotterdam Marathon three times between 1997 and 1999. She won New York in 1994 and 1995 and Berlin in 1999. Then she won London and Rome in 2000 and Lausanne in 2002.

In 2003, Loroupe followed her passion for peace and founded the Tegla Loroupe Peace Foundation. She also has successfully brought members of warring tribes together. To further this work toward peace, she founded the Peace Race in 2006, which included two thousand warriors from six different tribes.

"I grew up in a pastoral environment where life was really hard because of the local conflicts between the tribes and people stealing cattle. All of this on top of conditions that were hard to start with," she said, "I was lucky. I had talent and was able to make a success out of running and I felt that I wanted to give things back to the community I grew up in."[4]

In 2006, Loroupe was named a United Nations Ambassador of Sport. She is also a member of the "Champions for Peace," a group of athletes seeking to use the power of sports to bring about peace in the world. Tegla has also worked hard to advance the opportunities of Kenyan women.[5]

ANNIKA SORENSTAM (1970–)

Born October 9, 1970, Annika Sorenstam is a Swedish golfer with eighty-nine worldwide wins and seventy-two Ladies Professional Golf Association (LPGA) titles. Some consider her the greatest woman to ever play golf. Not only was she named the Rolex Player of the Year a record eight times, she also held the lowest seasonal scoring average six times on the LPGA Tour. What's more, Sorenstam won ten majors and earned an astonishing $22 million in her career.

But it was in 2003 that she made history when she played in the Colonial Tournament. She became the first woman to play in a PGA Tour event since Babe Didrikson Zaharias in 1945.[6]

A few of the male golfers expressed displeasure. Most notably, Vijay Singh, number seven in the world, told the Associated Press, "It's just different for ladies to play on the men's tour. It's like letting the Williams sisters play against

Annika Sorenstam brought attention to the sport of golf when she crossed over from the LPGA to the PGA to compete in a men's tournament. The ensuing controversy reminded many that misogyny still exists in the sports world.

a man, and they're far better athletes." He then added that he'd refuse to play with Sorenstam should he be paired with her. "She doesn't belong out here," he said.[7] But not every tour pro felt that way. For instance, Phil Mickelson said, "Guys who are having a tough time with this are thinking this is the men's tour. It's not. It's the best tour, for the best players in the world."[8]

Just like Babe Didrikson, Sorenstam was both Scandinavian and an all-around athlete. In addition to playing golf, she also played tennis, skied, and played football. Plus, she reigned over the LPGA just the way Didrikson had. Before she ever teed off at Colonial, Sorenstam had already logged five majors and five Player of the Year Awards.

At Colonial, her partners, Aaron Barber and Dean Wilson, both said they were honored to be in her group. They also worked very hard to make her feel comfortable especially because there were so many who did not feel she should be playing in the tournament. Early on, her nerves were apparent. But once she got them under control, she played well. But her score could have been even better if she made a few more putts.

The next day, though, Sorenstam did not do as well. She shot a 74 and missed the cut by four strokes. Historians note that after she sunk her last putt, tears filled her eyes. She had a lot to be proud of. Not only had she finished better than thirteen male golfers, but she won over quite a few critics. She showed the world that women can compete with men. Years later, Sorenstam was asked what she thought about her experience playing in the tournament. She had this to say: "I cherished the opportunity and tried to make the most of it," she said. "Hopefully, people will think that I represented myself, the LPGA and women athletes in general fairly well."[9]

DANICA PATRICK (1982-)

Danica Patrick, born March 25, 1982, in Wisconsin, grew up in Roscoe, Illinois, and began racing go-karts as a child. From 1992 to 1997, she won numerous regional titles. She also won the World Karting Association Grand National Championship in 1994, 1996, and 1997.

Initially, Danica was active in her school community and participated in a variety of activities including being a cheerleader. But eventually she felt called to follow her passion. She dropped out of high school to pursue her racing dream and later completed her GED instead of finishing high school.

Eventually, Patrick moved to Europe to compete in the cutthroat world of European road racing. After spending the 1998 and 1999 seasons driving in the British Formula Vauxhall series, Patrick moved to the British Zetec Formula Ford series for 2000 and 2001.

People first began to take notice of Patrick in 2000 when she finished second in the Formula Ford Festival. Bobby Rahal, a three-time Indy Car Series champion and an Indy 500 winner, in particular was intrigued by Patrick. He signed Patrick to drive in the United States for his team, Rahal Letterman Racing (RLR). As a result, she opened the 2002 season by winning the professional portion of the Toyota Pro/Celebrity race from the pole at the Long Beach (California) Grand Prix.

Patrick competed in the Toyota Atlantic Series in 2003. She became the first woman to finish on the podium, taking third-place at the road course in Monterrey, Mexico. She finished the year sixth in points, with an impressivefive top-five finishes.

By 2005, Patrick was gaining notoriety. For instance, in her debut at the Indianapolis 500, she became the first woman to lead a lap. But she did not just lead one lap. She held that lead for nineteen laps. She also posted the fastest lap on the opening day of practice, a feat that she repeated five times throughout the month.

What's more, her practice lap of 229.880 mph was the fastest of any driver during the month. It was also the fastest lap by any woman in the history of Indianapolis Motor Speedway. When it was all said and done, she qualified fourth. This starting position was the best ever by a woman. She went on to finish fourth, which was the best ever for a female driver.

In 2007, Patrick switched to Andretti-Green Racing and had eleven top-ten finishes that year. By the end of the season, she was in seventh place in the season-ending point standings. Despite her success, though, she had not made it to victory lane. It was only a matter of time.

By 2008, she won her first IndyCar race when she took first at the Japan 300. She also made history that day becoming the first woman to win an IndyCar race.

In 2010, Patrick started exploring stock-car racing even though IndyCar was still her primary focus. By 2012, she took on a full-time stock-car schedule. She competed in the Xfinity Series for JR Motorsports and raced in ten Sprint Cup competitions for SHR.

When she completed her first full season of Sprint Cup racing in 2013, everyone knew who Danica Patrick was. At the Daytona 500, she won the pole by setting the fastest time in qualifying and then finished eighth in the race, the highest finishing position ever for a woman in the "Great American Race." She also led the race for a number of laps. The only other woman to lead laps in a Sprint Cup race is Janet Guthrie. Guthrie led five laps under caution in 1977 at Ontario (California) Motor Speedway.

Early in the 2015 season, Patrick set a new mark for the most top-ten finishes of any female in Sprint Cup competition. She logged a total of six top tens. Janet Guthrie previously held the record with five top tens. Patrick went on to finish twenty-fourth in the driver point standings, her highest result.[10]

GABBY DOUGLAS (1995–)

Gabrielle "Gabby" Douglas enjoyed trying to copy her sister's gymnastic moves at a young age. Eventually, her parents signed her up for formal gymnastics training at just six years old, when her older sister urged her parents to do so. Born on December 31, 1995, Gabby had won a state championship by the time she was eight. By 2010, her family recognized her potential to be a great gymnast with proper training. They allowed Gabby to move away from her hometown and family to train with world-renowned Olympic trainer Liang Chow. Liang was best known for helping American gymnast Shawn Johnson become a world champion and Olympic gold medalist.

It wasn't long before Douglas was making her mark on the gymnastics world. At the Nastia Liukin SuperGirl Cup that same year, she placed fourth all-around. She also placed third on the balance beam, sixth on vault, and ninth all-around in the junior division of her first elite meet, the CoverGirl Classic.

At the 2010 US Junior National Championships, Douglas took the silver medal on balance beam and came in fourth all-around. She then won the uneven bars title at the 2010 Pan American Championships. She also took fifth all-around and won a share of the US team gold medal at that event.

The astonishing Gabby Douglas became the most decorated African American gymnast at the 2012 summer Olympic Games. Douglas went on to win another gold, in the team event, at the 2016 Olympics.

At the 2012 Olympics, sixteen-year-old Douglas became the first African American gymnast in Olympic history to win the all-around title. She was also the first American gymnast to take home the gold in both the individual all-around and team events. Later that year, she became the fourth gymnast to be named the Associated Press Female Athlete of the Year.[11]

MISSY FRANKLIN (1995–)

Melissa "Missy" Franklin was born May 10, 1995, in Pasadena, California, and grew up in Centennial, Colorado. Because her mother was afraid of the water, she made sure that Missy learned to swim at age five. She did not want her daughter to fear water like she did.[12]

This decision to introduce her to the water at an early age proved to be a wise one. By the time Missy was thirteen, she emerged into the national swimming scene at the 2008 Olympic trials. Although she did not qualify that year, she made a name for herself in the pool.[13]

In 2009, Franklin competed in her first international event, Duel in the Pool. And in 2010, Franklin won multiple medals at the world championships. It was the first time she would stand on the podium in international competition. She was also named Breakout Performer of the Year at the USA Swimming gala, Golden

Fifteen-year-old Missy Franklin astonished swimming fans by bringing home five medals at her Olympic debut in 2012.

Goggles. In 2011, she completed in her first long course world championship meet and nabbed five medals—three of them gold—and broke her first world record at the FINA World Cup.[14]

At the 2012 Olympics, Franklin took home an astonishing four gold medals and a bronze. She also set the world record in the 200-meter backstroke and 400-medley relay. Her five-medal haul was the most by any female competitor in the London Olympics. It was also the second overall highest medal count. American swimmer Michael Phelps collected six. In 2013, Franklin became the first woman to win six gold medals at a single world championship.[15]

BETHANY HAMILTON (1990–)

When someone mentions the name Bethany Hamilton most people think about the inspiration of hope she provides to millions of other young athletes. Despite being injured during a shark attack, she never gave up on the sport she loved. Instead, she found ways to continue pursuing her passion for surfing and competing against others.

Born February 8, 1990, in Hawaii, Bethany began competitive surfing at just eight years old. By the time she was nine, she had earned her first sponsorship. She also proved that she was capable of beating more experienced surfers in competition.

Despite losing an arm during a shark attack, Bethany Hamilton continued to compete in surfing competitions. Her grit and determination prove that women athletes have the power to inspire the world.

For instance, in May 2003, she won both her age group and the open division of Hawaii's Local Motion/Ezekiel Surf Into Summer event. Shortly afterward, she finished second in the open women's division of the National Scholastic Surfing Association (NSSA) National Championships at San Clemente, California.[16]

Her career was just getting started when tragedy struck. In 2003, when she was just thirteen,

Hamilton was attacked by a fourteen-foot (four-meter) tiger shark. Despite the heroic efforts of her friends, she lost an arm that day. Many in the surfing community believed this tragic accident would end her career as a rising surf star. But Hamilton had other plans. Just one month after the attack, she returned to the water.[17] She showed the world that losing an arm, although shocking and horrific, was not going to define her. She had every intention of fulfilling her surfing goals.

Although her road to success had some bumps along the way, Hamilton persevered. It was not long before she won the Explorer Women's division at the 2005 NSSA National Championships.[18] And in 2007, she realized her dream of surfing professionally. She placed second in the ASP World Junior Championships in 2008. Meanwhile, her story has been told in a *New York Times* best-selling autobiography and in the 2011 film *Soul Surfer*.

Hamilton is involved in numerous charitable efforts, including her own foundation, Friends of Bethany. This foundation reaches out to young amputees. But her desire to bring hope to others does not end there. Hamilton's latest project, *Surfs Like a Girl*, is a surf film, which will showcase her as one of the best women surfers in the world. Hamilton continues to touch and inspire lives globally as a professional surfer and motivational speaker.[19]

MO'NE DAVIS (2001–)

In August 2014, thirteen-year-old Mo'ne Davis became the first girl to ever win a game in the Little League World Series (LLWS). As the pitcher for her Philadelphia team, she led the Taney Dragons to a 4–0 victory over a team from Nashville, Tennessee. Many attributed this success to her 70-mile (112-km)-per-hour fastball.

Born on June 24, 2001, Mo'ne, is a multisport athlete who, despite her success on the baseball field, claims basketball is actually her favorite sport. In fact, she played on the high school girls' varsity basketball team even though she was only in eighth grade. She also played on the all-boy Anderson Monarchs baseball and basketball teams. Mo'ne has already racked up a number of awards even though her athletic career is just getting off the ground. For instance, she was the youngest player ever named the AP Female Athlete of the Year. She was also selected as Sports Kid of the Year by *Sports Illustrated.*[20]

CONCLUSION: CARRYING THE TORCH FORWARD

Although there has been a long history of discrimination against female athletes around the world, women have challenged the status quo and pushed for more opportunities. They have also fought for fair treatment and equal pay. Today, physical strength and athletic prowess are starting to be included in the world's concept of femininity. As a result, traditional beliefs about women are slowly disappearing. Now, female athletes are more empowered than they have ever been.

There is still some distance to cover, but it is clear that women are on the path to breaking free of the stereotypical demands. Female athletes are establishing themselves in the sports world and doing amazing things. It has been almost fifty years since Title IX opened the floodgates for female athletes everywhere. It will be exciting to see where the next fifty years take women in sports.[21]

CHAPTER NOTES

INTRODUCTION

1. "She's a Girl! So What?" Women's Sports Foundation, http://www.womenssportsfoundation.org/home/research/articles-and-reports/equity-issues/so-what-shes-a-girl.
2. "Report: Kicker Dismissed by Georgia Team for Being a Girl," ESPN, August 31, 2008, http://espn.go.com/college-sports/highschool/news/story?id=3560929.
3. "Women, Gender Equality and Sport," United Nations, December 2007, http://www.un.org/womenwatch/daw/public/Women%20and%20Sport.pdf.
4. "What Every Athlete and Parent Should Know," Girls First, http://girlsfirst.info/why-2/.

CHAPTER 1. THE HISTORY BEHIND THE FEMALE ATHLETE

1. Kristin Wilde, "Women in Sport: Gender Stereotypes in the Past and Present," Centre for Interdisciplinary Studies, http://wgst.athabascau.ca/awards/broberts/forms/Wilde.pdf.
2. Ibid.
3. Ibid.
4. Maria Popova, "Wheels of Change: How the Bicycle Empowered Women," Brain Pickings,

https://www.brainpickings.org/2011/03/28/
wheels-of-change-bicycle/.

5. Wilde.

6. Ibid.

7. "Women, Gender Equality and Sport," United
Nations, December 2007, http://www.un.org/
womenwatch/daw/public/Women%20and%20
Sport.pdf.

8. Ibid.

9. Ibid.

10. Ibid.

11. Ibid.

12. Ibid.

13. "What Every Athlete and Parent Should
Know," Girls First, http://girlsfirst.info/why-2/.

CHAPTER 2. HISTORY OF THE OLYMPICS AND WOMEN

1. "Ancient Greek Women in Sport," Elmira
College, http://faculty.elmira.edu/dmaluso/
sports/greece/greecewomen.html.

2. Steve Wulf. "Hey Fellas, Wanna Play Some
Ball?," ESPN, June 11, 2102, http://espn.
go.com/espnw/title-ix/article/8024358/
women-test-mettle-vs-men.

3. "Ancient Greek Women in Sport."

4. Wulf.

5. "Case Study: Female Participation in the Olympic Games," Learning Legacies, February 2010, https://www.heacademy.ac.uk/sites/default/files/cs12_womens_participation_in_the_olympic_games.

6. Ibid.

7. "Women, Gender Equality and Sport," United Nations, December 2007, http://www.un.org/womenwatch/daw/public/Women%20and%20Sport.pdf.

8. Team USA: Rio 2-16 Olympic Games, http://www.teamusa.org/Road-To-Rio-2016/Team-USA/Fun-Facts.

9. Victoria Patterson, "The First Female Olympians," September 25, 2013, http://the-toast.net/2013/09/25/first-female-olympians.

10. "Women at the Olympic Games," Top End Sports. http://www.topendsports.com/events/summer/women.htm.

CHAPTER 3. FEMALE ATHLETIC PIONEERS OF THE 1800s

1. "Alicia Meynell, The First Woman Jockey in England," History and Other Thoughts, http://historyandotherthoughts.blogspot.com/2014/11/alicia-meynell-first-woman-jockey-in.html.

2. Ibid.

3. Evans, Mary. "A Jockey Named Mrs. Thornton," *Sports Illustrated Vault*, December 2, 1968, http:// www.si.com/vault/1968/12/02/551275/a-jockey-named-mrs-thornton.

4. Ibid.

5. Ibid.

6. "Ellen Hansell Biography," International Tennis Hall of Fame, https://www.tennisfame.com/ hall-of-famers/inductees/ellen-hansell/.

7. "Ellen Hansell," Sports Pundit, http:// www.sportspundit.com/tennis/ players/7113-ellen-hansell.

8. "Ellen Hansell Biography."

9. "Ellen Hansell."

10. Nutt, Amy. "Wimbledon's First Wunderkind," June 14, 1993. http:// www.si.com/vault/1993/06/14/128771/ wimbledons-first-wunderkind-in-1887-lottie-dod-15-became-the-youngest-player-to-win-the-womens-title-at-wimbledon-she-still-iS.

11. "Lottie Dod–First Teenage Tennis Prodigy," Tennis Forum, http://www.tennisforum. com/59-blast-past/420732-lottie-dod-1871-1960-first-teenage-tennis-prodigy.html.

12. Ibid.

13. "Lottie Dod Biography," International Tennis Hall of Fame, https://www.tennisfame.com/ hall-of-famers/inductees/lottie-dod.

14. Ibid.

15. "Lottie Dod–First Teenage Tennis Prodigy."
16. Ibid.
17. "Lottie Dod Biography."

CHAPTER 4. MAKING HISTORY IN THE EARLY 1900s

1. Steve Wulf, "Hey Fellas, Wanna Play Some Ball?" ESPN, June 11, 2102, http://espn. go.com/espnw/title-ix/article/8024358/ women-test-mettle-vs-men.
2. Ibid.
3. Ibid.
4. "The Girls of Summer: Jackie Mitchell," Exploratorium, https://www.exploratorium.edu/ baseball/mitchell_2.html.
5. Ibid.
6. Wulf.
7. Ibid.
8. "Fanny Blankers-Koen," Encyclopedia Britannica, http://www.britannica.com/ biography/Fanny-Blankers-Koen.
9. "Fanny Blankers-Koen," The Official Website of the Olympic Movement, http://www.olym-pic.org/fanny-blankers-koen.
10. "Fanny Blankers-Koen," Encyclopedia Britannica.
11. "Alice Coachman," New Georgia Encyclopedia, http://www.georgiaencyclopedia.org/

articles/sports-outdoor-recreation/
alice-coachman-1923-2014.

12. "20 Inspirational Female Athletes Who Won
… In a Man's Sport," Sports Management,
http://sportsmanagementdegree.
org/2010/20-inspirational-female-athletes-who-
won-in-a-mans-sport.

13. KerriLynn Engel, "Fanny Sperry Steele,
Award-Winning Rodeo Performer,"
Amazing Women in History, http://
www.amazingwomeninhistory.com/
fannie-sperry-steele-rodeo-performer-cowgirl.

CHAPTER 5. BRINGING ABOUT CHANGE FROM THE 1950s TO THE 1970s

1. Barbara Winslow, "The Impact of Title IX,"
Gilder Lehrman Institute of American History,
https://www.gilderlehrman.org/history-by-era/
seventies/essays/impact-title-ix.

2. "Gender Biases in School," The Feminist eZine,
2001. http://www.feministezine.com/feminist/
sports/Gender-Biased-Sports-in-School.html.

3. Winslow.

4. Ibid.

5. Emma Cueto, "Becky Hammon and
12 Other Female Trailblazers in Sports
That You Should Know About," Bustle,
July 23, 2015, http://www.bustle.com/

articles/99373-becky-hammon-and-12-other-female-trailblazers-in-sports-that-you-should-know-about.

6. "Althea Gibson," History Channel, http://www.history.com/topics/black-history/althea-gibson.

7. Peter Dreier, "Billie Jean King and Remarkable Success of Title IX," *Huffington Post*, June 24, 2012, http://www.huffingtonpost.com/peter-dreier/billie-jean-king-and-rema_b_1621359.html.

8. "Billie Jean King," National Women's Hall of Fame, https://www.womenofthehall.org/inductee/billie-jean-king.

9. Ibid.

10. Steve Wulf, "Hey Fellas, Wanna Play Some Ball?" ESPN, June 11, 2102, http://espn.go.com/espnw/title-ix/article/8024358/women-test-mettle-vs-men.

11. Ibid.

12. Jesse Greenspan, "Billie Jean King Wins 'Battle of the Sexes,' 40 Years Ago," September 20, 2013, http://www.history.com/news/billie-jean-king-wins-the-battle-of-the-sexes-40-years-ago.

13. Dreier.

14. "Donna de Varona," National Women's Hall of Fame," https://www.womenofthehall.org/inductee/donna-de-varona.

15. "Wilma Rudolph," Tennessee History for Kids, http://www.tnhistoryforkids.org/people/wilma_rudolph

16. Ibid.

17. Ibid.

18. "Influential Women and Moments in Sports History," ESPN, http://espn.go.com/espnw/news-commentary/slideshow/10533618/3/wilma-rudolph.

19. "Kathrine Switzer," New York Road Runners Hall of Fame, http://www.nyrr.org/about-us/nyrr-hall-of-fame/kathrine-switzer.

20. "Nadia Comaneci," Bio, http://www.biography.com/people/nadia-comaneci-9254240#synopsis.

21. Wulf.

CHAPTER 6. LEVELING THE PLAYING FIELD: FROM THE 1980s TO THE 1990s

1. Betty Spear, "A Perspective of the History of Women's Sport in Ancient Greece," http://library.la84.org/SportsLibrary/JSH/JSH1984/JSH1102/jsh1102f.pdf.

2. "Influential Women and Moments in Sports History," ESPN, http://espn.go.com/espnw/news-commentary/slideshow/10533618/10/pat-summitt.

3. Mike Organ, "Legendary Lady Pat Summit: Pride of Cheatham County," *The Tennessean*, April 9, 2014. http://www.tennessean.com/story/sports/college/2014/04/05/

pat-summitt-tennessee-womens-basket-ball-ncaa-legendary-lady/7347089.

4. Ibid.

5. "Joan Benoit: First Woman to Win Olympic Gold Medal in the Marathon," About.com Education, http://womenshistory.about.com/od/trackandfield/a/Joan-Benoit.htm.

6. "Jackie Joyner Kersee," About.com Education, http://womenshistory.about.com/od/jackie-joynerkersee/p/joyner_kersee.htm.

7. Ibid.

8. "About Nancy Lieberman," Nancy Lierberman.com, http://www.nancylieberman.com/about.

9. "Mia Hamm," Bio, http://www.biography.com/people/mia-hamm-16472547#olympic-gold.

10. "Venus Williams," Bio, http://www.biography.com/people/venus-williams-9533011.

11. "Serena Williams," Bio, http://www.biography.com/people/serena-williams-9532901#personal-life.

CHAPTER 7. CARRYING THE TORCH FORWARD IN THE NEW MILLENNIUM

1. Amanda L. Abad, "Title IX Leveled Playing Field for Women Athletes but Not for Female College Coaches," *The Southwestern College Sun*, October 19, 2012, http://www.theswcsun.com/

title-ix-leveled-the-playing-field-for-women-athletes-but-not-for-female-college-coaches.

2. "Female Athletes Are in a League of Their Own," Imperial Health Center for Orthopedics, http://centerforortho.com/specialties/Sports-Medicine/Sports-Injury-Articles/Female-Athletes-are-in-a-League-of-their-Own.

3. Abad.

4. "Tegla Laroupe," Biography Online, http://www.biographyonline.net/sport/tegla-loroupe.html.

5. Ibid.

6. "Influential Women and Moments in Sports History," ESPN, http://espn.go.com/espnw/news-commentary/slideshow/10533618/13/annika-sorenstam.

7. Jerry Potter, "Singh Says Annika 'Doesn't Belong' on PGA Tour," USAToday, May 12, 2003, http://usatoday30.usatoday.com/sports/golf/pga/2003-05-12-singh_x.htm.

8. Ibid.

9. Steve Wulf, "Hey Fellas, Wanna Play Some Ball?" ESPN, June 11, 2102, http://espn.go.com/espnw/title-ix/article/8024358/women-test-mettle-vs-men.

10. "Danica," The Official Website of Danica Patrick, http://danicapatrick.com/danica.

11. "Influential Women and Moments in Sports History," ESPN, http://espn.go.com/espnw/

news-commentary/slideshow/10533618/15/
gabby-douglas.

12. "Missy Franklin," Bio, http://
www.biography.com/people/
missy-franklin-20903291#early-life.

13. "Influential Women and Moments in Sports
History," ESPN, http://espn.go.com/espnw/
news-commentary/slideshow/10533618/16/
missy-franklin.

14. "Missy Franklin," Bio.

15. "Influential Women and Moments in Sports
History."

16. "Bethany Hamilton," Bio. http://www.biogra-
phy.com/people/bethany-hamilton#!.

17. Bethany Hamilton Profile, Bethany Hamilton
Website, http://bethanyhamilton.com/profile.

18. "Bethany Hamilton."

19. Bethany Hamilton Profile.

20. "Influential Women and Moments in Sports
History," ESPN, http://espn.go.com/espnw/
news-commentary/slideshow/10533618/17/
mone-davis.

21. Kristin Wilde, "Women in Sport: Gender
Stereotypes in the Past and Present," Centre
for Interdisciplinary Studies at Athabasca
University, http://wgst.athabascau.ca.

GLOSSARY

Achilles tendon The tendon that connects the calf muscles to the heel.

arthroscopic surgery When an arthroscope is used to perform minor surgery on a joint.

autoimmune disorder A condition in which a person's immune system attacks the body's own cells, causing tissue damage.

bloomers Nineteenth-century women's clothing consisting of loose trousers that buttoned at the knee or ankle.

chauvinist A male who criticizes women based on the belief that females are inferior to males and therefore do not deserve equal treatment.

discrimination Unjust or prejudicial treatment of different categories of people based on gender, race, religion, or age.

empowerment To give power or authority to a person to improve upon self-esteem and belief in his or her abilities.

equality Having the equal rights, social status, and opportunities as others.

heptathlon An athletic event comprising seven different track and field events; it is won by the person with the highest total score.

intercollegiate Events or activities taking place between two or more colleges or universities.

loophole Ambiguity in a set of rules that allow participants to participate because it is not formally forbidden.

revolutionize To bring about radical change.

sharecropper A farmer who gives a share of his or her raised crops to a landowner in lieu of renting the land.

sidesaddle A saddle designed so that the rider sits with both legs on one side of the horse; these saddles were used by women wearing long skirts.

stereotype A negative opinion that is applied to a group of people based on their gender, race, or religion.

suffragist An advocate for female voting rights.

tethrippon A type of chariot horse race held in ancient Olympic Games.

Title IX A law passed giving women equal rights in sports and academics.

tsunami A large ocean wave caused by an earthquake or volcano that erupts under the water; the wave washes onto the shore and causes destruction.

women's movement A movement to give women equal rights in education, sports, and employment.

BOOKS

Blumenthal, Karen. *Let Me Play: The Story of Title IX: The Law That Changed the Future of Girls in America*. New York, NY: Atheneum Books for Young Readers, 2005.

Bryant, Jill. *Women Athletes Who Changed the World*. New York, NY: Rosen Publishing, 2012.

Egendorf, Laura K. *Girls and Sports*. Detroit, MI: Greenhaven Press, 2012.

Finch, Jennie, and Ann Killion. *Throw Like a Girl: How to Dream Big & Believe in Yourself*. Chicago, IL: Triumph Books, 2011.

Gitlin, Marty. *Billie Jean King: Tennis Star and Social Activist*. Edina, MN: ABDO Publishing, 2011.

Rappoport, Ken. *Ladies First: Women Athletes Who Made a Difference*. Atlanta, GA: Peachtree Publishers, 2010.

Samuels, Mina. *Run Like a Girl: How Strong Women Make Happy Lives*. Berkeley, CA: Seal Press, 2011.

Stabler, David. *Kid Athletes: True Tales of Childhood from Sports Legends*. Philadelphia, PA: Quirk Books, 2015.

WEBSITES

Girls Inc.
girlsinc.org
Girls Inc. is a mentoring program designed to encourage leadership and empowerment in girls.

National Women's Hall of Fame
womenofthehall.org
The website of the Seneca Falls museum contains important historical information of the women's movement.

Official Website of the Olympic Movement
olympic.org
The official website of the Olympic Games

Women's Sports Foundation
womenssportsfoundation.org
Billie Jean King founded this organization in 1974 to ensure that girls would have access to sports.

INDEX